CHAPTER ONE

TERNION PATHS

CHAPTER ONE

TERNION PATHS

CARLOS FABELA

Ternion Paths: Chapter One

ISBN: 978-0-578-94185-1

PROLOGUE

"Thunder Makes Not Lightning"

Fat drops of rain had made the weathered and abused concrete slick and dangerous as she made her way down the desolate collection of empty storefronts. Her breath came in shallow gasps and she tried to hold herself upright, her fingers searching for holds in the old brick and mortar of the long-since-failed dream of an entrepreneur.

She leaned heavily against the wall while cradling her pregnant belly and staring up at the roiling black sky, at clouds angrier than she imagined they could be. The thunder shook and rattled the windows above her. It was as though nature itself was loudly protesting this moment.

"Please . . . just a bit more time." She begged her exhausted body forward and another crack of thunder startled her sideways toward a car and she fell to her knees.

She wrapped her fingers around the door handle and willed herself back up. A small kick moved deep in her belly as life and energy flowed back into her limbs. Warmth gushed into her chest, beating back the cold—but something was wrong.

Comfortable warmth turned to feverish heat as she leaned against the old station wagon. Her heart lurched when the vehicle inexplicably shuddered to life, lightly idling at first but revving until the engine was roaring and straining.

She stumbled away from the screaming steel shell as the engine, fueled by some unseen force, continued rising in power and noise. Taking refuge behind an upturned dumpster, she could only sob and clutch her belly while the noise reached a crescendo that echoed off the streets.

The vehicle's metal body began to glow red and then exploded with a deafening crunch that shook the nearby concrete as shrapnel flew off and embedded itself in the surrounding buildings.

The dumpster rocked from the force but managed to protect the woman from flames and flying steel. She peered around the rim and found the vehicle gone. Only scorched asphalt and broken glass gave any indication it had been there at all.

Desperate to get out of the storm, the woman made

her way inside an old pawn shop the blast had unlocked by destroying the door. She huddled low and hid in a dark corner in case the explosion drew the wrong kind of attention, which was typical for this part of town.

The heat inside in her belly churned and spread through her arms and legs. *This doesn't feel like the contractions the doctor from the clinic described.*

Where were the birthing pains, the water break? Why couldn't she remember how she had come to this desolate, forsaken place?

Plaster and mortar powder drifted down onto her head, breaking her thoughts. It fell silently against the noise of the relentless storm. She peered through the gloom of the old shop and realized the dust was coming from everywhere. The walls of the old building were beginning to disintegrate.

As the heat inside her grew, the tingling began.

Tiny sensations of static discharge grew into unbearable jolts of pain, and all the while, the walls and ceiling were crumbling, larger chunks of plaster now freeing themselves and thudding down around her. An old light bulb on a nearby shelf began to glow and hum.

She stared intently at it, not knowing what to expect of anything around her. Everything had been unexpected since the beginning of this pregnancy.

The bulb's hum became louder as it began to wobble. Frantically, it bounced around before the light inside flared with brilliance and the bulb shattered.

The light in the room, however, did not dim.

She searched for the new source of light illuminating the room, but it was not until she looked down at her own round belly that she realized the glow was coming from her stomach.

All her doubts, all her rationalizing, fled in that moment as she admitted the truth of her unborn child's connection to the odd happenings around her.

Uncomfortable heat prickled her skin as the glow began to spread.

The debris and abandoned items in the pawnshop around her started to gently shake and move as though caught in an underwater current.

She closed her eyes, pleading for time to move slower.

*

The dark swirling clouds ceased their wrathful show of noise and wind. They quickly dispersed—leaving the sun free to try and spread hopeful rays over a new scar on the ground.

A smoking hole obscured by gently wafting debris and ash floating back down to earth was all that was left of an old pawnshop.

*

"Cheryl . . . Where's your car?" Mona asked, voice oddly hushed.

Cheryl continued following her friend's light footsteps, oblivious to their surroundings as she dug through a purse for her keys.

"Right where I parked it, Mona. Nobody would want to steal that piece of—" Her snippy remark died on her lips as she stopped hunting for her keys in her purse and looked to where Cheryl's gaze was frozen.

It was not hard to piece together what had happened.

Her parking space was missing the car she had left there that morning. The spot was now occupied by a large black scorch mark. The damage of a blast was obvious from the walls and broken windows near where they had left the vehicle, but as they approached, Cheryl noticed a gap from the completely missing building. Mona burst into a run.

"What the hell are you doing, Mona?" Cheryl shouted after her.

Cheryl then heard what had started Mona sprinting—an infant's distressed cries faintly winding their way out of the smoking ruin.

CHAPTER 1

Dave adjusted Ann's coat, straightening the collar while checking the dark gray fabric for smudges and rips. The coat was obviously too big for her, ill-fitting and designed for an older woman.

"I guess we beggars can't be choosers," he muttered under his breath.

A few seconds passed before Ann's small voice rang out clear. "What did you beg for?" the six-year-old asked earnestly.

Dave smiled, surprised she had heard him but knowing better from past experience than to show it. He stood straight once again, unsatisfied with the fit of the coat but helpless to change it.

"Let's see," he thought aloud with mock seriousness. "Well, I begged the placement center to spend the day with the prettiest and sweetest girl in the world!" He grinned and lightly bopped her nose with his finger.

Ann's small face could only manage a forced and dispirited half smile, and it broke his heart. His grin slowly left his face leaving only a smile he refused to drop, if just for her sake. "All right, let's go then."

*

Pulling up outside the beautiful house in his barely running junker, Dave watched as Ann stared in awe—and perhaps a little fear. Dave, too, had been impressed with the huge, lavish home and lush manicured lawn. One look around at the other houses, however, exposed a neighborhood of carbon-copy homes and shiny cars. Dave wasn't sure if the uniformity gave the neighborhood an oppressive feel, or if this was the normal atmosphere and it was simply in the character of such people to demand uniformity, but either way his heart sank a bit.

This house would be the twelfth adoption interview for Ann, when most of the kids in the group shelters went to bed praying for just one. Finding permanent homes for the displaced children of Fenny had always been difficult—even more so since the city had begun a decline fueled by drug cartels and the violence that was never far behind them.

Consisting of upper-class families and sitting on the outskirts west of the harbor, this subdivision was one of the few neighborhoods that remained a bastion of prosperity and safety in Fenicia. The fact that a large percentage of the already scarce police force was posted here, leaving the poor and more dangerous parts of the city to fend for themselves, spoke of the influence the well-off of the city could afford.

While permanent homes had become scarce for the orphans, foster families were usually not in short supply thanks to the checks paid out to the willing temporary caretakers. For some in the city, this was their only source of income, their homes becoming revolving doors of nameless faces. Most kids would simply be bounced from foster home to foster home until they reached eighteen, when the city's understaffed and underfunded Department of Children's Services was forced to throw them to the streets, only to have their futures inevitably devoured by the gangs.

Ann's dark brown eyes narrowed doubtfully in the direction of the house, betraying a similar line of thinking to Dave's.

"Hey," he said, breaking the silence.

Her head turned slowly, her eyes last to leave the house.

"Guess what happens," he jerked his thumb towards the house, "after this."

Slowly but surely the edges of Ann's mouth turned up.

“Ice cream,” she whispered, speaking the word with reverence before slapping her hand to her mouth.

Department rules were very clear about potential adoption visits, and side trips for ice cream were not in the manual. But Dave always found his own little justifications for breaking the rules, not that it was difficult.

Ann was such a sweet girl with deep dark-brown nearly black eyes, her light blond hair and light skin contrasting dramatically against them. The couples that came in always fell in love with her as soon as they spotted her.

Dave only wished that whatever drew them to her would stick around. Every time he thought he had placed Ann permanently, he would without fail receive the call. Like clockwork, the adopting couple would back out of the process, returning Ann to the department’s lobby completely against protocol simply to be rid of her. With the lobby in a completely different building from the group homes, Ann was left to be looked after by the front-desk staff for the hours it took to get a ride back for the girl.

It was after her third adoption return that Dave met Ann in the lobby. Having been headed out to lunch that day, he asked the receptionists about the little girl flipping through magazines in the lobby and upon hearing how she was unceremoniously dumped in front of the building, he volunteered to take her back to the group home, treating her to lunch on the way. Ann and Dave had struck a fast friendship, and he found himself determined to find her a home. He immediately put in his request to be her placement worker, her first words to him echoing in his memories.

"No one wants me."

Giving Ann one last look-over on the sidewalk, he noticed one of her sneakers was loose. He bent and tied a proper shoe knot.

"There, picture perfect," he declared.

She smiled, giving her foot a wiggle to test the tightness before giving him an exaggerated nod of approval.

Turning towards the house, he offered her his open hand. "Ready?"

Her nervousness was apparent to him through her continued silence, but Ann nodded yes and took his hand as they began up the walkway. Dave felt her squeezing hard, her small hand gripping tighter in fear the closer they got to the front door.

I hate this, he couldn't help but think to himself. *Putting her through this over and over again.* He wished he could adopt her himself, but the income from his Placement Department job wasn't near enough to meet the income qualifications for adoption.

Dave knocked on the center glass pane of the finely

carved wood door, waiting a few moments in the quiet of the neighborhood. Though it was thick and frosted for privacy, the glass was still opaque enough to see shapes and shadows inside. He watched as a blurred figure quickly made their way down the stairs. As the moving shadow inside reached the door, he heard two heavy lock bolts slide free, and a harried-looking woman in her late forties swung open the front entrance.

Powerful physical locks were all the rage these days among the affluent, replacing the high-tech computer security systems in an odd reversal of progress. A string of rather high-profile break-ins had caught the attention of anyone who had been using computerized security systems, the hacking perpetrator having made short work of even the most advanced systems.

While the woman must have been beautiful in her early years it was apparent that an obsession with youth had driven her to the knife. Her face reminded Dave of puzzle pieces that didn't quite fit together. She wore what might pass for a nightgown but for the slitted sides and plunging neckline exposing her stomach.

Dave found her appearance odd. The woman was breathing rather heavily, and there were sweat spots beginning to show through the fabric of the gown.

"Yes?" Her impatience was obvious. She noticed Ann at his side and frowned, displeased at the interruption.

"I'm sorry, I don't want any cookies . . ." Her tone was cold and she was about to close the door when Dave stammered a few confused words and began flipping through his folder of paperwork. He wondered if perhaps he had gotten the wrong home or address. After all, wouldn't people remember a midday adoption interview?

"I helped make cookies once!" Ann excitedly piped up, trying to engage the woman who might be her new family.

"We had to mix the—" she began excitedly before being sharply cut off.

"That's nice. Can I help you?"

Ann closed her mouth immediately, eyes downward as her hand again squeezed Dave's as hard as she could.

Dave stammered through a few words until the woman's eyes narrowed in anger and impatience.

"Adoption? I'm sorry, you must have the wrong house." She took a step back and began to shut the door.

Having continued reading through his paperwork Dave finally located the name he had been searching for.

"Schneider? Thomas Schneider?" he blurted through the remaining crack of the closing door.

The door stopped, reversed, and swung open again. "Yes, that's my husband." she said slowly, confusion and worry etched on her face.

Before Dave could reply, the sound of a roaring engine echoed down the quiet street, stealing their attention. A brilliant red sports car sped toward them. Barely slowing, the man driving jerked the wheel and skidded into the driveway before touching his brakes, the car coming to a screeching halt accompanied by thick black tire marks.

Figuring this to be Thomas, Dave began turning towards him only to notice the woman's face locked in panic. Though it took a few seconds she managed to get a hold of herself.

"Honey!" she yelled much too loudly. "What are you doing home?"

What on earth is going on? Dave wondered, flinching from the woman's volume. He thought he heard a loud thud come from somewhere upstairs, but couldn't be sure. One look at the driver told Dave that the screamed welcomes were not the norm.

"Traffic. So sorry. Tried to hurry." He huffed while making his way to them.

He struck Dave as your average business type, though his clothes had seen better days. The cuffs of the shirtsleeves and slacks were beginning to fray. The man spoke to Dave, but his eyes were focused on his pale wife as he grinned from ear to ear. "It was supposed to be a surprise, honey. We're parents now!"

The silence that followed seemed to stretch into minutes. Dave was absolutely floored by the situation unfolding. He couldn't help but wonder who he just heard upstairs if this was Thomas.

"What did you do?" the woman asked incredulously, her voice low and dangerous.

"I know I was fired, Sara. And you have been so distant, so I just thought we should finally be a family. I thought it would bring us together. I told them you work odd hours but would be here for the interview. Honestly, they seemed too slammed and short on people to question me."

Dave looked at him incredulously. How had this situation passed through the normal interview and adoption processes? "Wait a minute. You wanted a kid to fix your marriage? And this was a secret from your wife?"

Before Thomas had a chance to respond, they all heard the sliding back door roughly pushed open, followed by the heavy thudding of a large man tripping. A male voice cursed followed by a groan.

Peering over at Thomas, Dave noticed the man's face was now clenched and turning a light shade of red. "Who's here, Sara? There shouldn't be anyone here . . ." He practically growled, shoving past her into the house.

Dave grabbed Ann's wrist, pulled her close and

walked away from the house towards his car. "This is our cue to leave, sweetie."

The loud commotion from back inside the house followed them. Dave heard Sara's voice clearly in the calm of the afternoon. "You were fired, Thomas. I have needs!"

Dave buckled Ann into the passenger seat before making his way to the driver's side of the car. Shutting the car door, he silenced the domestic dispute for the both of them. They sat quietly for a few moments as he digested what had just happened.

Starting the car, he pulled into the street and began heading up the road. Dave gripped the wheel tightly and couldn't help but feel heartache for the poor girl as she continued to stare out her window silently. "Ready for some ice cream?" he asked, hoping to get something, anything, out of Ann after that scene.

She didn't answer, her wet eyes focused on the speed-blurred landscape passing by.

"I told you I would find you a home, Ann. But not that one." They drove, the silence soon becoming comfortable between the two.

Pulling into the gravel lot of Ann's favorite ice cream shop, Dave found a space thanks to the weekday afternoon lull. It was a small fast-food stand, the dine-in area consisting of a few weathered picnic tables spread out haphazardly around the gravel lot. The kiosk offered the basic staples of frozen milk confections and roller hot dogs.

Normally, Ann loved nothing more than to sit at her favorite table, especially when it was full. He often wondered if it was just the ice cream she loved about this place, or if it was also the attention and affection she received from strangers waiting for their desserts.

This is not one of those days, thought Dave as they stood waiting at the service window for the two cones he had ordered.

Recent heavy rain had flooded the lot, leaving most of the tables sitting in inches of water, including Ann's favorite faded pink table. Dave loved the history it held for the two of them. He always brought crayons with him so she could doodle on it while enjoying her treat. The first picture that started the tradition was still preserved there, the crayon lines strangely not fading even after all this time.

Ann had been eyeing their usual spot since they arrived, her face pinched and upset. She said nothing, but he could easily enough guess that the flooded picnic table was a terrible end to a bad day. He knew there was no way for him to move the substantial solid-wood and steel by himself.

Taking the two cones from the preoccupied cashier,

an odd sensation flooded him, the hairs on the back of his neck standing on end.

She was no longer next to him.

Shuffling on the gravel he turned to his car. “Ann?” he said, voice rising, but she was nowhere near the vehicle.

“I’m sitting right here,” she said absentmindedly, doodling on the faded pink table that now stood on dry gravel, several yards from where it had been.

He noticed deep trenches where the thick legs had dug into the wet gravel and earth.

Reaching up for her cone, Ann stayed focused on her drawings, giving Dave a distracted thank you as he handed it to her.

“How did . . .” The question started then died on his lips as he thought better of asking it.

Besides, she never knew when asked, and it almost always upset her to be pressed for an answer.

CHAPTER 2

Large flakes of snow danced and twirled on a light wind, obscuring the trail of crunched white powder she had been following. Shoving her loose blonde bangs back up into her winter cap, Cheryl let out a deep sigh and continued trudging away from the chimney smoke rising into the gray sky behind her. She remembered how quickly she used to run out of breath in Fenicia, but out here, the fresh air beckoned her out for a walk nearly every day. Squinting back behind her, she noticed the fat flakes were falling faster and faster, and she could barely make out the smoke now. The tracks were nearly filled in by the snow.

"What are you thinking, Nius?" she whispered into the silence that covered the pine woods like a thick blanket before continuing to walk in the direction the tracks led. Carefully picking her way through the lily-white snowfall and dark raised tree roots, her eyes scanned for anything that could be a sign of his presence.

She didn't know what she was looking for, but she would know when she saw it.

After a few more minutes of trudging she let out another sigh, this one of relief. She made her way toward a copse of trees that had caught her eye. As she got closer, she could see why. While the quickening pace of the snowfall was making it harder to see everywhere else, there were portions of those trees that were hidden in a dense roiling fog.

Relieved she had found him so close to the cabin, she made her way towards the wall of shifting mist, stopping just short of entering. She slipped off her gloves and tucked one into each pocket before unbuttoning her thick winter coat. Cheryl stepped into the thick fog surrounding the group of trees.

Immediately there was warmth of a balmy spring day, and not a trace of snow. Cheryl breathed deep, filling her nose with the sharp smell of pine needles and moist earth.

"Nius?" she asked, her voice seeming to disappear in the mist. "The snow's picking up. I'm getting worried . . ."

"About me?" came the questioning response from directly above her.

"No, about the trees. They'll start thinking its spring if you keep hanging around them like this," Cheryl said with a smile. She heard his laughter somewhere in the tangle above her.

"It wasn't like that a minute ago."

Peering through the mist and branches, she tried to listen and pinpoint where he was, but to no avail. "Penny for your thoughts?" she nudged. It usually didn't take much to get him talking to her.

After Mona had died, just before Nius's eighth birthday, Nius had clung to Cheryl like a frightened kitten. It was rare for him to be out alone like this. She wanted to chalk it up to regular teenager behavior—he was soon turning sixteen after all—but deep down she was uneasy with the rationalization in that answer.

She fumbled in the pocket of her draped coat, past the glove, and found a small worn travel Bible. Mona had read to him from it since the moment he could talk. Cheryl supposed old habits died hard as Mona had been a nun in her early years. That was before they'd met—when they were both in their early twenties, Cheryl older by a year. Though Mona never spoke of having left the convent, she also never stopped reading her Bible and praying.

The seclusion of their lives in the woods had afforded Mona the ability to not be frequently asked the questions people generally did. Folks were always demanding to know how she jived her religion with her life and love. Though the move from Fenny to the country had originally been for Munius, the two women could not have been happier. Gardening the rich earth around their cabin gave them delicious produce. They learned to preserve in jars for the winter months, and had built a makeshift greenhouse with some old windows to extend the growing season. Though they were only thirty minutes away from the nearest town, they had found the spaces between visits growing ever longer.

This was perfectly fine as far as Mona had been concerned. Introductions to townsfolk could eventually lead them to questions about Munius. The women knew that even a casual look into the boy's past would raise red flags.

The worn leather of Mona's pocket Bible felt odd in Cheryl's hand. Nius had carried it with him since Mona's death. When he had turned twelve, Nius began reading it hungrily and daily. Cheryl had never really been able to pinpoint the reason for the dramatic change. For the last few years, she had rarely seen him without his nose in it. But recently he seemed to carry it more out of habit, never cracking it open.

So when Cheryl found it on the kitchen table without

him, it was enough to send her bundled up and out into the cold.

"I miss her," he said softly above her.

Her fingers traced the embossing of the pocket Bible, gold color peeling away like dry paint.

"I miss her too, Nius . . . A whole lot."

A soft creak sounded from a branch above her followed by the quick rustle and rush of smaller twigs and dry leaves. Cheryl looked up and caught sight of his sneakers through the swirling fog. Her heart caught in her throat as she watched him fall like a stone about to crash down. Plummeting feet first through the branches, Nius suddenly slowed his descent just inches from the wet earth.

One dirty sneaker touched down lightly and Nius stepped forward with the other foot, closing the gap between him and his mom.

Cheryl sucked in a deep breath, realizing she had stopped.

"I don't think I will ever get used to that, Nius." Cheryl stared up at where he had dropped from.

Still miles away, Nius barely registered what she said. "Yeah, I won't ever get used to her being gone either."

After a moment, he noticed her peering up into the swirling fog he had dropped from. "Oh, you mean *that*."

"Yes, *that*," she said, drenching the last word in sarcasm. "The whole flying thing, you know?"

"I don't fly," he said simply, following her gaze up into the tree before looking back at her with a frown. "I don't actually DO anything . . ." he muttered, his face showing signs of the frustrations welling within.

Cheryl knew where this was going. "Fine, then, the not-crashing-into-the-ground-after-falling-thirty-feet-like-you're-supposed-to thing."

He smiled, the traces of frustration disappearing.

To Cheryl and Mona, finding him in the still smoldering ruins of that old abandoned pawnshop had seemed to be the weirdest thing about him at the time. She remembered how they had made their way through the wreckage, following his cries before finding him swinging his tiny balled fists with gusto and crying as hard as his little body could muster.

*

"What happened, Mona? We were only gone for an hour . . . Where's your car? Where's his mom? Where's the building?" she finished loudly, beginning to feel pangs of hysteria.

Reaching down, Mona attempted to slip her hands under the infant and lift him into her arms.

She gasped loudly, a burning pain igniting the back

of her hands. "Ow, he's lying in burning embers!" She reached down again, quickly grabbing him and lifting him up and out of the smoldering remains of the building. Cooing and holding him tight, Mona tried to comfort him.

"Cheryl, check his back. How bad is it burnt?"

Cheryl tried to answer but could not, uttering a soft noise before stopping. She tried again with the same result.

"Cheryl, he needs us. He needs you! Please, pull yourself—"

"He's fine Mona. His skin is perfect." Mona sighed and pulled him closer, kissing his cheeks. His cries were quieting.

"Your hands, however, look like raw hamburger, love," Cheryl said grimly.

Mona was completely oblivious to her surroundings as she clutched the boy close. After a few silent moments passed, the gravity of the situation clutched Cheryl again.

"We have to call someone, Mona. He looks fine but he really should be looked at."

Mona began shaking her head no as soon as Cheryl started speaking, sucking any real conviction out of the sentence.

Cheryl took a guarded glance around, struck by

something odd. "Where is everyone? There are no police, no ambulance, no city workers . . ."

Mona didn't respond, her hands working to remove her shirt and wrap the warm cloth around the child.

"No junkies, no homeless people, no crazies claiming to be a sewer-grate god," she finished, squatting down next to Mona.

The boy had stopped crying as soon as Mona had held him close. He smiled up at them and began kicking his legs, almost as if hoping to move closer.

Cheryl smiled curiously at the boy. He looked tiny. She would honestly have guessed he was a newborn, but his eyes were wide open and alert, and they tracked her easily.

"We have to take him, Cheryl. Look around you." Mona motioned at the destruction all around them. "There is no one here for him. Just us."

Cheryl was aghast that the conversation was actually heading in this direction. "That's kidnapping, Mona! It's a crime, with consequences. It's not like we found a kitten in a trashcan. He's a baby. He could have fami—"

An odd look came over Mona's face. Her eyes were bright and excited, and her smile was barely contained by her mouth. The building momentum of Cheryl's lecture was stopped dead.

"He didn't burn," Mona practically whispered, beaming down at the child. She looked back at Cheryl, eyes full of determination. "He's not like us, and you know it." Mona angled the badly burned and bleeding backs of her hands up at Cheryl to press the point.

*

Cheryl knew Nius loved and usually trusted her enough to tell her anything.

Anything except of course for what had been bothering him recently. It was an awkwardness that both had begun to feel.

"Sure you don't want to talk?" she pressed hopefully.

"Yeah, we can talk. About what?" Nius answered brightly, deflecting the question.

Cheryl ignored his deflection. "Walk me home? Or should I put my coat back on and say a goodbye to these trees?"

Looking in the direction of the cabin, he rubbed his stomach in hunger.

"Definitely, what's for dinner?"

"I don't know, dear. What were you planning on making?" Cheryl grinned at him and started walking. Her boots made deep prints in the mud as she disappeared into the mist and back towards the cabin.

*

"Do you think I'm an angel?"

Cheryl stayed quiet, spending a few moments thinking. Dinner had been quiet and the silence unnerved him. She answered slowly and deliberately at first, but gained momentum.

"Let's start with, 'I'm glad you felt like you could talk to me about this,' and second, 'I'm not mad at Mona even though I really don't agree with her on this.'"

He started to speak but she held up a hand to stop him knowing full well what was coming.

"You don't have to tell me what she said. I'm pretty sure I know. But I feel like I should get my two cents in."

She squeezed his hand tight.

"Angel, demon, saint, devil, leprechaun, Christmas elf. YOU decide and only you."

He looked unconvinced, but she continued. "Soon you're going to have to make your own path in this world, Nius, and it's going to be one never walked before. The choices and decisions you will have, others won't even be able to imagine."

Her stare had turned hard and serious.

"But if you go forward now, bound to what Mona said, chained to what she needed to believe, you will never find your own way."

Nius slumped in his chair, deep in thought. A few moments passed before he finally spoke. “Thank you. I think I’ll head to bed and read.”

*

Nius continued to fall backwards, as if he had been falling forever. Time and direction seemed meaningless in the absolute darkness. Panic gripped him. His mind was overwhelmed by a sense of immense inconceivable distance and his outstretched fingers found only emptiness.

Somewhere behind him a pale glow broke the darkness.

Nius tried to turn himself, to face the brightness, but found he could not.

The light pulsated in a steady rhythm.

He exhaled and noticed that the light dimmed. Then the glow flared brightly again as he inhaled.

It’s my breathing? He mulled this over, determined to turn and face the light source. He willed himself, gritting his teeth with fists clenched.

Just turn . . . His fall slowed then stopped, before Nius felt himself moving upwards.

The immeasurable cavern fell away as he rose toward the tunnel he had left just moments before. He reached out, the soft comforting walls close and rushing past him as he sped upwards, away from the glow.

A glow that he was slowly forgetting had been there at all . . .

He couldn't remember why he had wanted to turn so badly.

It must not be important, he thought to himself, breathing deep and letting himself go in the darkness.

Nius woke slowly, wisps of forgotten dreams fogging his thoughts as he floated gently.

Moonlight pierced the surface of the water; it was a shining orb distorted in the depths.

His body rocked lightly in the current, the heaviness like a blanket surrounding him.

Water? he thought curiously, still half asleep. Groggily he opened his eyes, the black-blue depths moving and bending the rays of moonlight.

Nius snapped fully awake in panic.

"WATER?" he tried to scream into the lake, issuing an assortment of gurgling noises and a heavy rising stream of bubbles.

Thrashing his arms, he righted himself and felt his feet kick up silt from the bottom of the lake. Nius pushed off the lake floor and began desperately swimming towards the surface. His lungs burned for oxygen and his fingers reached for the surface, but he knew he wouldn't make it.

Wide-eyed and panicked, he gave one last kick, thinking of Cheryl and Mona in his last few moments.

Unable to hold his breath any longer he sucked in.

Nius floated dumbfounded a few feet below the surface. The expected rush of water into his lungs was instead a deep breath of air.

Breaking the surface of the lake, he breathed the colder air in deep.

With skin and pajamas untouched by the frigid water, he scanned the shore, looking for any landmarks. At last, he spotted the familiar maple tree reaching out over the lake, unmoving in the cold, still night.

He pushed hard, kicking his way until he reached the edge of the lake. Pulling himself out of the water, Nius plopped down on the snow-covered shore.

The air surrounding him instantly rose to a comfortable temperature, the snow around him melting and leaving him sitting on the muddy bank after a few moments.

"What the hell was that?" he muttered as he stared out at the lake, its surface now calm.

While the family of three had grown used to the unexplainable happening around Nius, he had never encountered anything like this before. His mind raced as he tried to piece together what had happened, while simultaneously trying to wrap his mind around discovering he somehow breathed water.

He must have fallen asleep at his desk. After all, he didn't remember crawling into bed. It made sense. For the last few months he had spent hours at that desk in his room poring over books and searching the web.

But why, after falling asleep at the desk, had he woken up in the depths of the nearby lake?

"Who does that?" he yelled into the freezing night, angrily whipping a rock at the water.

He watched as the stone continued skipping out onto the lake until completely out of view, the sound of the skips getting softer until they disappeared.

He could practically hear Mona as he lost himself in thought on the bank. *We found you because we were supposed to,* she would say to him often. They had not been shy or secretive with him about how they had come to be a family. They always answered his questions honestly.

He knew they had found him in the rubble, knew how the burning ash that had left Mona's hands scarred had not touched him.

But for all he knew, he had no answers.

Now, standing on the muddy bank of the frozen lake surrounded by familiar and comforting woods, Nius began his strange walk home.

Clear and cloudless, the night did not feel like it harbored evil or ill will. Stars bright as beacons in the black sky shone down as he walked barefoot in pajamas and a t-shirt. Each step left a melted muddy print as he made his way to the cabin.

In the last few weeks, and after talking to Cheryl, Nius had finally begun to feel some control over his life and powers. The recent events had made sure to do away with that sense of control and ease.

CHAPTER 3

The sweat ran down Jim Mallon's face and mixed with his blood. He breathed as deeply as his broken ribs would allow before the pain caused him to pass out. He was bound tightly and had long ago lost the feeling in his hands. Even if he were rescued now, he was certain his extremities would never function the same. In fact, he suspected that's exactly why the bindings *were* so tight.

"Where is he?" Jim hollered to the empty room.

The loss of blood and the regular beatings made focus difficult and his mind wandered. Thinking back to that day, he could feel the panic as the memories flooded him. His mind replayed his own abduction over and over again.

The quickness and efficiency with which the armed men had rushed the police precinct parking garage was nothing short of devastating. That it was a brightly lit afternoon and no one stopped them was a slap in the face.

His once crisp black suit was now torn and ruined with large crusted stains revealing barely clotted wounds. It was the same suit he had been wearing two days ago when he had left work.

The memories infuriated him as his eyes attempted to pierce the darkness the solitary light bulb hanging above him could not.

"Can't handle me with a working trigger finger? Quit hiding you coward!"

Jim knew the room was empty, but he could pretty much guarantee his abductors were watching and listening. It was all the incentive he needed to keep shouting insults and threats. Rocking back and forth, he tried again to get some feeling back into his legs.

He had always realized this was a possible job hazard of being Chief of Police. Others had likened it more to a probability. Born into the poorer area of Fenicia north of the harbor forty-six years ago, Jim had always fought for what he felt was right. Mere hours after asking his high school sweetheart for her hand in marriage, he had followed in the steps of his hero and father. He'd joined the police force, where he rose rapidly through the ranks.

Jim loved the city and cherished his childhood

neighborhood right on the coast, just north of the largest port. His beloved neighborhood existed only in memories now. The last four years had been the worst, the downturn reaching a point of no return.

Breathing a heavy sigh, Jim noticed the force of his shouting had caused his nose to bleed again. He felt faint with unconsciousness and growled himself awake.

Most in the city simply called it a decline, but having been in law enforcement for these many years, Jim knew that decline was a terrible understatement. This city had been dragged kicking and screaming into the darkness.

He chuckled woozily to himself, the sound echoing menacingly in the dark room. He had to admit it had been orchestrated beautifully.

It had begun slowly. A small string of "corrupt cops" had been prosecuted and jailed by some guy called Olevot, the new head of internal affairs. The trickle of corruption became a stream as officers higher and higher up in the police force began being implicated and jailed. They claimed innocence but the public outcry was deafening. News outlets simply encouraged the irrational anger as their ratings soared, regardless of details and facts. Before long, even Fenicia's mayor found his poll numbers dipping in the wake of the arrests.

Jim was admittedly taken in by the hype against the

force. Using the public's momentum against "corruption" and his distinguished record he climbed his way up the emptying ladder. It didn't take long before he finally reached the big desk of Chief of Police.

The city knew and loved him enough to temporarily quiet the building storm against the city's police. With this access to the internal affairs records, he imagined his answers would be forthcoming.

But they simply created more questions.

What bothered Jim the most as he read through the cases and trial records was that in some instances, the search warrants predated the starting dates of the internal affairs investigations.

How were the courts issuing search warrants before the investigations even began, let alone actually finding evidence? Inquiries to the court for answers were met with a ridiculous runaround before he was eventually informed that it must have been a computer error.

With such an unsatisfactory answer, the tiny seeds of conspiracy began to sprout. Jim Mallon, however, was not one to simply give in to paranoia.

He needed real answers.

Unfortunately, the majority of his days had been spent defusing manufactured scandals as the city's love for him waned. The city's anger even cost Mayor

Russell his reelection bid to a heavily financially backed opponent.

While Jim felt the newly elected mayor might need to be looked into, he found himself powerless. Even his warrant requests were now being systematically denied by the courts. *Someone high up has to be involved for so many warrants to be denied and so many convictions to be sped through the system*, Jim thought.

Not only did he not have access to the needed court information aside from trial records, but nearly half of his force was behind bars. Short on officers and high on crime, Jim Mallon began taking daily beats himself, right on the streets like his fellow officers.

The exhausting work of covering shifts for so many was draining and robbing him of time with his family. He had begun to feel like the last breakwater before a tsunami.

Then the new recruits arrived, and Jim began to seriously worry.

Clean cut and sharply dressed they came. They carried an air of either complete indifference or hidden machinations, and they all seemed to be very tight with Olevot. The precinct felt like a viper pit. Jim was constantly interrupting private conversations that were instantly dropped when he came within earshot.

As angry as he was about his fellow officers standing

down and doing nothing as they watched him being taken, he couldn't say he was surprised.

Bound in the dark room, Jim froze. Not taking so much as a breath, he strained to catch the sound again. It was gone, and he was unsure if he had even heard it.

The faint slap of hard shoes on slick floors made its way down the narrow hall toward him.

"Great," grunted Jim sarcastically. "More visitors." His body tensed, abused muscles aching in anticipation.

CHAPTER 4

"I think someone can't keep their eyes off of you," Dave said with a smirk as he swung his leg over the seat and sat down at the table. He set down the ice cream sundae and pushed it towards her.

Ann dragged the plastic dish in front of her and dug in with her plastic spoon. Her gaze remained fixed on the hazy Fenicia skyline in the distance. She waited a few seconds before finally answering after her first bite.

"I know. I was going to go talk to him," she scoffed.

"Think he's cute?" Dave asked.

Ann's eyebrows arched, her face more annoyed than anything. "I think he's rude." She took a quick glance back at the ice cream stand. "Staring is rude."

Sure enough, the young man was still looking over at their table. Seeing Ann glance at him, he leaned against the service counter to give a little wave that she ignored.

"Oh, come on," Dave said with mock exasperation.

"He was a nice kid. He treated you to that ice cream, you know."

Ann began pushing the frozen treat away but Dave's hand stopped the plastic dish.

"Fine, I bought it. You got me."

"Good. Guys who believe they deserve something from girls they think are pretty tend to be bad news." Then she grinned. "And don't mess with my ice cream!" She playfully pointed her finger at him, prompting him to put his hands up before biting into his cone.

Looking back down at the table, his eyes traced the hundreds of little doodles left by Ann and a crayon over the years. Now sixteen, her desire to color on the pink table had pretty much evaporated.

The happiness and ease he felt with those memories disappeared as the weight of his current problems settled back onto his shoulders.

While it may have signaled the end of her table-doodling aspirations, Ann turning thirteen a few years ago had also occurred around the time that Father Gene had begun requesting possible adoption interviews at his beautiful home. It was a thought that terrified Dave.

Roughly five years ago, Father Gene had been chosen as the replacement priest of the Charleston suburb church after the untimely death of Father Orland. His handsome features and golden eyes made him an instant hit, especially with the young members of the congregation. Unmarried, he lived by himself in his large home in the beautiful suburbs of Charleston, and he frequently spoke of the joy of adopting.

With his reputation and following growing every day, Father Gene had even begun visiting the Placement Center regularly. He spent hours scanning through the pictures of orphans. Dave and the other workers were excited by the possibility of an adoption by the seemingly kind priest.

Dave involuntarily shuddered in the cool afternoon, angry at his own past naivety.

Father Gene's first adoption was a young girl named Lindsey. Dave hadn't been the placement worker for her, but he did remember the girl. And he damn well remembered her disappearance.

He remembered Father Gene's tearful pleas on the local TV stations, begging Lindsey to come back home and saying that he would forgive her for running away. The rest of the community grieved for Father Gene's lost runaway lamb, but Dave thought it suspicious.

Lindsey had always been a quiet girl with a huge thirst for reading. She sometimes had to be prodded just to get her to leave her books and come to mealtimes. Her running away just didn't make sense to Dave.

After digging through her adoption follow-up papers, Dave was infuriated to find what he thought were surefire signs of abuse right there in the report. They mentioned her drawn pale appearance, large bags under her eyes, withdrawn behavior and no eye contact. In the report, Father Gene explained them as the signs and symptoms of mono, which the placement worker obviously accepted.

Dave tried to force the issue and get the police to pay some attention to what Father Gene was doing but he always hit a wall of influence and money. His higher ups and their higher ups kept shutting down his claims against the beloved priest.

But when Father Gene's next adoption of a young girl named Gabriela also resulted in her "running away," Dave's superiors finally acted. They suspended adoptions to Gene's estate while they agreed to investigate wrongdoing, but no one expected the decision to be struck down by Fenicia's government officials.

Eight children in the last five years had been adopted by Father Gene. All had allegedly run away, never to be found again. By that time, however, Father Gene's church following had swelled. His congregants lapped up his excuses about the missing adoptees, always blaming them for their own disappearances. He would explain in his honey-sweet manner that it was because he searched out the most disturbed and misbehaved children to attempt to save.

It was an absolute lie that filled Dave's throat with bile as he thought about Gabriela and Lindsey and the others. But the church and community ate up the charismatic lies and excuses.

Dave pushed himself up from the table and tossed his cone in the garbage. He arched his head back to stop the wetness forming in the corners of his eyes and looked up at the clouds. Taking in the cool air through his nostrils he let out a defeated sigh. The dark gray sky threatened rain, but that seemed to fit his mood.

He looked over at Ann. It was hard not to worry about her. Dave couldn't blame her for her disinterest in people. As a child she had been very outgoing, always trying to chat up anyone who stopped to listen. But that part of her was gradually crushed by people's fear of what they did not understand. Friends especially had always been a touchy subject for the girl. In more recent years, she carried herself with a stoicism and toughness that made it clear she didn't need them.

But Dave knew better, knew that the toughness was a protective shell. *I just wish she could meet someone her own age to talk to, a friend to tell the things she can't tell me.*

He looked back at her as she slowly lifted spoonfuls

of the fudge-melted vanilla ice cream to her mouth. She kept staring out at the city's skyline in the distance.

"Ready to go home?" he asked, eying the clouds that threatened to soak them.

The two could turn just about anything into a cause for ice cream, but today marked eight years that Ann had a home. Though Dave never made enough money to legally adopt her, the center knew they needed to do something. By pulling some strings, they assigned Dave foster home status, with no intent of changing it until Ann was out of the system.

It had taken years, but Dave had finally found her a home—his.

The wind picked up, blowing Ann's long blond hair into her face. She swiped it away with her fingers and rubbed her napkin across her mouth. "I was hoping we could go to the city?" she questioned. Her eyes were hopeful as she looked at him.

Looking towards the car, Dave smirked.

"I can't help but think I should have expected this."

Ann surged ahead with her carefully planned defense of her proposal.

"Listen, we can stick to Main Street and catch a movie. Then we can eat at that place we always pass with the golden-colored dragons. We won't be anywhere near the dangerous parts, I swear!"

Dave began to open his mouth to speak but Ann beat him to it.

"And I won't wander off," she finished with a smile.

"That's nice but—" Dave began, but Ann interrupted again.

"And we won't stay late!"

Dave shook his head with a grin, revealing to Ann that she had cracked his resolve. He knew full well he was caving, but he couldn't deny her. Not today.

Downtown Fenny was a safe tourist destination with a nightlife hotspot for those who could afford it. There was simply too much money to be made for the city to let any sort of undesirable element near the brightly lit and beautiful Main Street area. Everywhere else, though, was a slum. The harbor and surrounding areas were a beast that appeared to be trying to find a foothold into the rest of the city, crime and gangs festering.

"Well, let's hurry then. I'm starving and that Chinese is sounding great compared to cold ice cream." Pulling his smartphone out of his pocket he handed it to Ann. "I'll go pay for these cones. Wait for me in the car and figure out which movie you want to see."

Ann reached for the phone but then stopped. "Didn't you already pay? You're not still trying to get me to talk to that kid, are you?"

This time it was Dave who gave her an exasperated

look. "Just go wait for me. I only want to ask him if there is still construction down Lake Street."

"Ok . . ." Ann let the word hang as she trudged towards the car.

Dave approached the young man and shook his head apologetically.

"Sorry, kid. She's not interested." He slid the price of Ann's ice cream towards the dejected-looking boy and then walked back to the car. He pulled his old junker onto Lake Street and headed north towards downtown Fenny with her.

*

Ann watched the landscape stretch and grow as they neared. Small homes and neighborhoods gave way to the immense steel and concrete towers of the city. With its huge stretch of shops, restaurants, theaters, nightclubs and culture, Main Street was unmistakably the heart of Fenicia. Ann had fallen in love with the bustle and atmosphere of life here.

Dave watched as Ann craned her neck to stare up the sides of the beautiful buildings. The huge panes of glass reflected the mix of colorful lights that bathed everything in glow.

He knew she fantasized about her future life in one of the decadent penthouses in the buildings towering above her. She wanted to wake up in a beautiful bedroom before getting ready for work somewhere glamorous and important in the city.

Absent mindedly her fingers wrapped tightly around the door handle.

"Easy there, Ann." Dave teased and nodded toward the handle. "Don't want you accidentally rolling out."

She let it go, grinning sheepishly before turning again to watch the busy streets.

Dave turned off of the main street and pulled up to the automated pay parking machine. Ann hopped out of the car before he'd even shut down the engine.

"Hey now!" Dave shouted after her from inside the car as he undid his seatbelt and grabbed his keys. She was already around on his side of the car opening the door for him.

"Today, Dave! I promised not to stay late, but you're eating into our time!"

"I'm not eating into our time yet. Just wait until we're at the restaurant," he joked.

They made their way to the packed intersection outside the garage. Joining the group waiting for the light to change, they took in the city.

They both inhaled deeply as they walked past an Italian bakery, the sweet and herb smells merging a few steps away with the aroma of hazelnut and coffee.

A steady flow of patrons streamed in and out of the packed cafe with smiles and steaming drinks.

"Want some coffee?" Dave asked, pulling her up to the end of the line.

He knew coffee in all its delicious forms was practically her blood type. Though he was also aware that it was also about the caffeine and avoiding sleep. Nightmares and terrible memories always seemed to find her, just like they had last night.

"Your usual order then?" Dave asked.

"Uh, yeah. Mocha espresso, three extra shots, please," Ann blurted, snapping back to the present.

"You planning on sleeping?" Dave kidded, unsuccessful at disguising the concern in his voice. "Ever?"

She made a face at him, but she couldn't hide the flash of worry.

"Let's have a seat." Dave nodded toward the less occupied area of the coffee shop near the bathrooms. "All right . . . How about we just skip the part where you pretend everything is ok to make me feel better, and save some time so we don't miss the movie."

Ann was a bit miffed for a second but gave in with a sigh of relief. "I was just remembering my first adoption."

"The Macianis? I wasn't on that case, but I remember reading the case files."

*

The Maciani couple had no children of their own, which made Giovani Maciani thoroughly ashamed, as the case worker noted in the file. Had Dave been working the case, he would have flagged that up with his superiors, but not everyone was so thorough.

He and his wife had accused Ann of demolishing their house, though Dave knew better.

He'd been able to get the story from Ann in bits and pieces over the years.

*

"You see that?" Giovanni had said importantly to five-year-old Ann as they entered the Macianis' home. Unable to contain his pride in his enormous flat-screen television set, he clicked the remote and brought the TV to life.

"Clearest, sharpest picture around. The black is true black. Stand next to it; get a feel for how big that picture is."

Ann frantically shook her head no, afraid of the large and intimidating man. She wished his wife Marissa were here to help. Giovanni roughly grabbed Ann's arm, having mistaken her fear for insubordination, and move-shoved her toward the television.

"This, Ann," he brought his face close to convey his seriousness, nodding towards the TV. "This you don't ever touch."

He stopped abruptly, looking uneasy and tense as he watched her. Giovanni licked his dry lips and stared at Ann. He narrowed his eyes at her suspiciously, then shook his head dismissively, when a blinding white arc of electricity leapt from Ann to the television screen.

The television's sound began to crackle with static as the voices bled together, becoming a loud screech. The odor of acrid burning plastic filled the room. Large cracks in the glass spread out from where the energy had struck, fracturing the screen like an intricate spider web.

As the small cloud of smoke cleared, a wide-eyed and slack-jawed Giovanni looked from the now destroyed television to Ann and back, his brain clearly trying to wrap itself around what had happened.

Marissa entered, spotted the now destroyed television and gasped in shock. "Did someone break in?"

Giovanni shook with rage. Face screwed in anger, he slowly stood and towered over Ann.

Ann remained absolutely still, a buzzing in her head growing louder as she felt weaker and weaker. She shut her eyes tightly, tears streaming down her face as Giovanni exploded into motion, grabbing Ann by the front of her coat and lifting her to eye level,

"Giovanni! Stop it! She couldn't have done anything!" Marissa screamed at the man.

Giovanni ignored her completely, lost in his anger. "You did that on purpose, didn't you?" he bellowed at Ann, but she refused to open her eyes.

Ann scrunched her face up tight, but remained quiet. Her silence only served to infuriate him further until he began to shake her in an attempt to force an answer. Ann squeaked at the painful jerks to her neck as her head swung violently back and forth. Marissa ran to them, attempting to free Ann, but with his free hand, Giovanni struck the woman away viciously.

Put me down, put me down, put me down, put me down, please put me down, *Ann silently screamed in her head.*

"Answer me! What did you do?" Giovanni demanded, but Ann said nothing, eyes squeezed shut.

Put me down put me down put me down, please please please **put me down.**

"What the—?" Giovanni grunted with effort as his arm slowly lowered, as if Ann suddenly weighed as much as a bag of cinder blocks. With his free arm, he grabbed the other side of Ann's coat and heaved up

with all his strength, but it did little to slow her descent to the floor as she grew heavier and heavier.

Her jacket finally ripped from the strain and she fell the last few inches to the floor, feet meeting the wood with an impossibly loud thud that cracked the planks beneath her and rattled the walls of the home. Structural beams and joists groaned loudly in protest at the immense stress.

Ann opened her eyes as soon as her feet hit the ground, revealing a splayed Giovanni clutching his wrist as he watched her with a primal terror in his eyes. Weakly he pushed with his legs, simply trying to get away from her.

Loud groans from the floor became a booming crack of wood as a beam snapped under her weight, the floor of the home dropping a few inches and tossing Marissa to the floor like an earthquake.

Instinctively wanting to help, Ann took a step towards Marissa, but the woman screamed in terror at the child.

"Stay away from me!"

Ann's small movement towards Marissa had caused the groaning of stressed supports to reach a horrible crescendo. With a thunderous crack, the few remaining beams finally gave out, and the entire room collapsed into the pitch black of the basement.

Marissa's screams being drowned out by the horrible noise were always the last thing Ann remembered from that day.

*

"She wasn't anything like him, you know? The wife."

"Melissa?"

"Marissa." Ann corrected, pensive.

Dave conceded the point with a nod and signaled her to continue.

"She was so nice to me, she was sweet. It just . . . It really seemed like she liked me," Ann finished, staring down and wistfully swirling the contents of her cup.

"Who is to say she didn't?" Dave offered.

"*She* said as much when I destroyed . . ." She paused, struggling to find the strength to begin the long story, but Dave held a hand up.

"I can pretty much piece together what happened to their floor, but what did she say exactly?"

Ann sighed and rested her chin on her sleeve-covered hand.

"You know, the basics. 'Get away from me, stay away from me, don't come near me.'" She held up her other hand and counted them off one by one with her fingers.

Dave laughed, and then looked apologetic. "Well it

sounds like she *did* care for you. But people aren't good with what they don't understand. You know that."

Ann began nodding in agreement before instead shaking her head no. "But why is that my fault? I can't control what happens around me." She finally blurted out the thoughts that had been eating at her as an anxious anger bubbled over. "Is the rest of my life going to be one long attempt to hide what I can do just so people don't hate me?"

"No," Dave said sternly. "Don't you change—"

Ann interrupted, unenthusiastically finishing the now familiar sentence. ". . . who you are for someone else. If they don't like and accept you for *you*, then they aren't worth it."

"But you'll never know who is who if you don't actually talk to them."

She wiped the corners of her eyes one last time, drained the last of her coffee, and stood up. "I'm ready to go now."

Dave rose, wrapped his arm around her shoulder and pulled her close in a half hug. "We are out there, Ann. People who can see how amazing you are. I promise."

She nodded half-heartedly as they walked out of the coffee shop and back onto the street.

Dave's phone buzzed and he glanced at the screen. "Looks like the news about Jim finally broke."

"Missing and presumed dead? That sucks. Jim always seemed nice enough."

Dave began looking behind them urgently. "We gotta go now, Ann. This is bad." She watched as the blood drained from his face. Dave's hushed and anxious tone frightened her.

He grabbed her wrist and began walking back the way they had come, in the direction of the parking garage.

"What's going on? What is it?" And after another moment, "Dave, WAIT!" she demanded, her voice rising.

"I promise that as soon—" He stopped when he noticed two men behind her heading directly for them.

"Dammit," he cursed as he turned.

Facing the approaching men, Dave reached out and grabbed Ann's hand, slowly taking steps back away from them.

"Ann," he whispered. "When I turn around—"

"I see your lips moving buddy," shouted the seedy-looking guy, interrupting him. "Don't do it. Don't you dare make a run for it!"

Dave simply squeezed her hand. "RUN!"

They both turned and began running as fast as they could away from the approaching thugs. Dave could hear their pursuers' footsteps getting closer, quickly gaining ground with the light rhythm of a practiced runner.

The men continued to gain ground until they were close enough to stop them. One kicked Dave to the ground, and the other one, sneering, grabbed Ann and spun her roughly to face him before slamming her head into the concrete wall of the building to disorient her.

"Guh." Ann groaned in pain as the back of her head connected with the rough concrete.

She tried to struggle but the thug held Ann by her throat and squeezed tightly so she would hold still. Dave could still not breathe and his head spun.

Ann's hand shot up to grab the man's arm in a futile attempt to pull his hand away from her throat.

"Ann, wait!" Dave whispered hoarsely, but he knew she could no longer hear.

A burst of hot blood sprayed out as an awful piercing shriek erupted from her assailant's mouth. The man clutched the bleeding stump that had been his wrist.

Ann slid down the wall in a daze, staring at her own blood-covered hand. Her would-be kidnapper was now rocking on the dirty ground, whimpering and clutching a heavily bleeding wrist.

The other man moved and jabbed a syringe in the back of her neck. Her eyes fluttered shut as the drug took effect. Dave, bound and gagged, had felt the sting seconds earlier. He tried to scream her name, to somehow convey that he'd fix this, that he loved her. He fought to keep his eyes open. Ann faded out of focus as he slipped under.

CHAPTER 5

Nervous perspiration made his grip slick as Onur fingered the ridges and nodules of the device in his palm, as if committing them to memory.

God, my ass is killing me, he thought. A full hour spent sitting in the cold shipping container had made his legs and butt painfully numb against the oddly ridged floor. With one hand, he worked a smartphone so quickly his fingers appeared to blur. His custom modification of green lettering on a black screen gave off very little light. Onur was pleased with the darkness.

Tapping anxiously against the floor with his foot he continued watching the dim screen for any updates.

His phone abruptly vibrated, haptic feedback quietly informing him it had illegally picked up a nearby text message from someone else. Immediately, he opened it and read, hoping desperately for some good news.

Hey Jon, he wants us to switch in ten minutes but I was hoping you could cover my shift tonight?

What? Onur thought, pondering the unexpected change. *Well I guess that's lucky . . .*

An idea began brewing in his mind.

Onur slipped the roundish steel device from his hand into his pocket and sat up. Navigating his phone, he found the application he was looking for. He initiated the custom program and waited a few moments before feeling the telltale vibration.

This time he knew he wasn't just spying on the private conversation, but intercepting the message completely so the other recipient would not receive it. He waited and without fail came the other man's response.

Seriously? I had to work in the rain all last week and I already covered two of your shifts. You are never able to cover mine, not to mention how last minute this is. It's raining tonight and I have plans, Carl. I can't cover for you.

That works, Onur thought.

He began typing his own replacement message before hitting send.

Fine fine, I will cover your shift. I had nothing going on tonight except for watching cable with my cats.

Onur laughed quietly inside the shipping container.

"Man, I hope things go this easily all night," he whispered, focusing on the task at hand.

"Ok, I've got ten minutes before the guard gets antsy," he said out loud.

"I sure am talking to myself an awful lot tonight," he mused with a nod.

"It's probably the nerves."

He rolled his eyes.

"Well, no shit it's the nerves . . ." he answered himself sarcastically before clamping his mouth shut.

Small rays of artificial light filtered in through the cracks as he slowly approached the doorway of the container. He grabbed the metalwork on the inside of the door and pushed it open a bit more, surveying the night outside. Dark clouds obscured the moonlight and stars high above, giving the entire area the cold wet smell of impending rain.

The large steel box sat in an empty field strewn with

dozens of rusted barrels and similar old shipping containers, far away from the main warehouse and security fencing that protected the area.

Though they looked like unassuming shipping containers, Onur knew they each contained an array of sensors intended to let warehouse guards know of any surrounding activity. The poor and homeless of Fenny were not picky when it came to shelter, regardless of the "No Trespassing" signs.

Onur had easily hacked the electronic feeds for the sensors in his own container, but he would need to be careful if he stepped near any of the others.

He spotted movement near the fence; a normal warehouse worker except for the fact that he carried a fully automatic assault rifle.

There he is. Jon the guard, waiting for his shift to end . . .

Before Onur took another step, he reached into his pocket and rolled the roundish metal device in his palm, anticipation and nerves eating at him. He scanned the field trying to find the best route to the guard but now felt woozy, nearly hyperventilating at the thought of actually rushing out there.

Looking towards the warehouse, he studied the hundreds of powerful lights that seemed to illuminate any of the possible nooks and crannies he might have used to sneak in. He could almost imagine the spray of bullets raining down on him as sirens blared, leaving him wishing for nothing more than to be safe and sound in his apartment.

Nah, he thought with guilt. *Jim wouldn't give up on me that easily.*

Imagining what the big guy might be going through inside the warehouse helped to steel Onur's resolve. He wrapped his fingers around the device in his pocket as he removed it.

"Now or never," he whispered as he waited for the guard to complete his perimeter walk and turn his back towards him.

The warehouse guard paused and pulled deep on his cigarette as he looked out over the garbage-strewn field and empty shipping containers. Exhaling into the cold night, he casually flicked the cigarette butt and ambled back the way he had come.

Onur slowly eased open the rusted door and stepped out onto the patchy grass and hard packed dirt. He took a slow steadying breath before sprinting up the hill towards the guard. He ran as quietly as he could, managing to get within fifteen feet of the armed man before the silent night betrayed his steps.

The guard took a drag from his newly lit cigarette. "You're early, Carl. Did you walk the perimeter to get out here?" The security guard asked into the night, not even bothering to look behind him.

Onur slowed to a casual walk and rolled the round-ish device around in his hand, fingers searching for the small button and pressing it.

Instantly, a high-pitched whine pierced the night, emanating from deep within the round metal ball.

"Nope, not Carl. Just breaking in," he cheerily answered the guard before whipping the metal ball as hard as he could at the armed man's back.

As the small metal sphere silently connected with the man, his body jerked cartoonishly and a heavy grunt escaped his lips. The guard crumpled to the ground, unconscious.

"Worked like a charm," Onur gloated before cautiously approaching the small metal device that had dropped to the ground beside the knocked-out guard.

He grabbed a twig off the ground and squatted down next to it, tapping the device a few times. Finally confident it would not shock him into a heap beside the unconscious guard, he breathed a sigh of relief and picked it up, slipping it into his pocket.

The capacitor is discharging beautifully. I should up the voltage.

He turned his attention towards the unconscious guard, rifling through the man's pockets.

"Come on, where is it?"

Not finding what he was looking for, he began to search around the man's belt, finding a large square box clipped to it. "Here we go."

Onur lifted the guard's coat and spotted an ID card tethered to a retractable leash belt clip to prevent it from getting lost. Pulling on it, he heard the clicks inside the square box as he freed more and more of the thin cable from the retraction mechanism.

From one of his other pockets he removed a multi-tool and angled the thin cable into the powerful wire cutters. About to squeeze and cut the cable from the retraction box he stopped; something in his subconscious was screaming at him.

He looked again at the cord, noticing it was indeed thicker than it should have been. Inspecting it more closely, he rolled it around in his fingers, noticing small white lettering in spots.

This isn't just a tether, this is an electrical cord.

He lifted the guard's jacket again, examining the retraction box attached to the man's belt, careful not to let it slip off. Suspicious, he pressed his hand against the side of the square box, feeling that it was much warmer than it should have been, almost hot.

It's a transmitter, he realized as he looked up

towards the warehouse with disdain. *Clever bastards! As soon as I snip that wire, I won't be able to swing a cat without hitting a guard, and I bet if I unclip it from him it's the same story.*

Without another wasted second, he took out his modified smartphone and held the ID card close, waited a few seconds. The phone vibrated and lightly beeped, letting him know the access information on the ID card had been wirelessly copied to the phone.

"Dammit," he whispered into the night in frustration as he stood up to get moving. *Only the newer doors are going to be wireless RFID. Everything else is going to need that damn card.*

"Oh well, no stopping now," he lamented.

He approached the chain-link fence and knelt down to keep his profile small as he reached into his other pocket and removed a small cordless Dremel tool. Not particularly large or powerful, it was similar to one that might be found in a hobby shop, except of course he had made special modifications to this one.

With his own blend of adhesive binder and grit along with a powerful corrosive, it made short work of just about every metal he had tested it on.

"Ok, girly, time to do your thing," he whispered as he flicked his phone back on and located the control program he needed.

"Position?" he questioned into the device, watching the screen for a response.

A virtual map of the area instantly popped up showing a small blinking dot a few feet from the perimeter fence on the other side of the facility.

"Switch to manual control."

The virtual map on his phone switched to a live camera feed. Near the bottom of the screen was a collection of small touch-screen toggles and controls. Carefully placing his thumbs on the screen, Onur began to direct the controls, biting his lip in concentration.

*

"Did you see that, Russ? Something's up there," Will whispered.

Russ responded by lying back on the concrete loading dock with his arms relaxed behind his head. "Dial it down a notch, man," he chided, thinking Will was simply being skittish, "There probably is something in that tree. Take your pick, squirrel, bird, raccoon."

Will relaxed his tensed trigger finger, shoulders slacking in relief.

"Yeah, you're probably ri—" he began before a sharp cry cut through the night.

"CAW!"

Russ sat up now, taking aim with his assault rifle.

The call from the tree had been oddly tinny and human sounding. "What in the hell was that?"

"I knew it!" Will scolded in anger, "You lazy ass, I told you something was up there."

Russ kept his eyes trained on the tree as he wrestled to find a clever retort. Before he could think of a witty rebuttal, something smallish and grey shot out of the trees.

"CAW!" came its cry again, strangely muffled and staticky. "CAW!"

With wings flapping madly, it flew in strange jerky circles, screeching out every few moments.

Russ eyed it curiously. As far as birds went, he had never seen or heard anything like it. Then again, he was no bird expert. His eyes followed its erratic flight pattern as he slowly stepped towards it.

"Is it drunk or something?" his partner questioned earnestly, but Russ's curiosity was becoming suspicion.

"Honestly, I'm not even sure it *is* a bird," he muttered quietly.

Without warning and with one last blared "CAW!" the feathered gray mass changed direction and plunged right into the chain-link fence. Tangled in the links, it continued to flap wildly, rattling and shaking the fence.

Immediately, the two men felt their communications devices vibrate as security personnel inside the warehouse attempted to inform them that something had triggered the fiber optic detection system on the fence.

"Yeah, yeah, we know, we know," Russ muttered into his walkie talkie as he approached the small creature cautiously, gun at the ready.

He turned to his partner, a puzzled look on Will's face.

"If that is a bird then it's the ugliest damn bird I have ever seen," he said while reaching out and plucking it out of the fence.

He examined the creature closely. It seemed to be made of some sort of light metal covered in feathers that had been haphazardly glued to the body. A crookedly glued plastic beak sat below googly eyes purchased from a crafts store.

Looking around for anything suspicious but finding nothing out of place, Russ turned to his partner. "Stay here and keep an eye out."

He looked back down at the small machine, turning it over in his hands.

"Boss is going to want to see this," he said grimly, not enjoying the prospect of being interrogated by his superior.

*

On the other side of the facility, Onur had already used the distraction and cut his way through the fence. He crouched near the building as he tried to plan his next move.

Well, first step was getting in, I guess, he thought as he sat amidst a collection of boxes and racked his brain. *My plan should probably have had a step two.*

He scanned around his hiding place and listened hard for anyone approaching as he eyed a locked entrance mere feet away. He shot out from his hiding spot and raced to the door, holding his phone against the wireless security panel reader. After a few seconds, a small green light lit up on the panel, followed by a small beep and click as the door unlocked. Quickly, he opened the unoccupied side entrance, hopeful that he had not triggered further security.

Onur found himself standing at the beginning of a dark stretch of hallway lit every few feet by not enough fluorescent tubes. *This feels a bit ominous.*

Eerie shadows melted and shifted in his peripheral vision as he made his way down the hallway. With smartphone in hand, he walked the straight forty feet before reaching a three-way branch of locked doors.

Argh! he thought, looking at the three doors. *This*

is all pointless if I can't get closer to the center of the building and pick up the signal.

He closed his eyes, focusing and picturing the spot where he had entered the building and how far he had walked. After combining it with his rough knowledge of the layout he dismissed the door to his left and in front of him. Those routes would only take him farther from where he needed to go. The door to his right was his best bet for picking up the signal he was so desperately searching for.

"And, of course, it's the one door of the three I can't open," he griped as he examined the card-swipe-dependent security panel. While the other two doors operated on wireless RFID technology that he could replicate and hack with his phone, this door would only open with an actual security badge.

He carefully sidled up to the door on the left and peered through the single pane of reinforced security glass, immediately ducking down to prevent being seen by the guard on the other side.

Perfect! He felt a devilish grin spread across his face as he formulated a plan to open the needed door.

Navigating his phone, he set a timer for the RFID-cracking application before resting the phone on top of one of the wireless security panel readers.

He began counting down the time as the phone's

timer ticked towards zero, taking the small ridged-metal sphere from his pocket and pressing the charge button. He placed it on the concrete floor in the center of the three doors as bait for the curious. The device's high-pitched charging whine resonated down the hallway and Onur sprinted back the way he had come, hoping enough distance and the extremely dim lighting would hide him from the guard's attention for long enough.

When he reached the end of the hallway he crouched down. *4, 3, 2, 1.* He held his breath as he finished counting down, focusing intently on the end of the hallway as the scene unfolded.

Even at this distance, he heard the quiet beep of the security panel as it denied his phone's binary dirty limerick with a red light and angry loud buzz that echoed down the hallway.

That was definitely loud enough to get his attention.

Sure enough, after a few seconds he heard a security panel beep once more, the right-hand door slowly swinging open as the guard cautiously investigated the corridor.

Come on. Go for the shiny metal ball. You know you want to.

The guard peered around the three doors, his glance finally resting on the small metal sphere in front of him.

Yes! Onur thought triumphantly as the guard knelt down and reached for the lure.

A small grunt escaped the man's lips as his body jerked and crumpled to the ground.

Cautiously approaching the knocked-out guard, Onur couldn't help but think he should really be hiding the trail of unconscious bodies he was leaving. If any of his handiwork was discovered, he had no doubt the facility would enter lockdown, and after that, even mice would find it nearly impossible to leave the building undetected.

With determination, he bent over the guard and grabbed the man's body armor straps. He heaved with all his strength, grunting and groaning but only managing to move the man a few inches before the effort forced him to gasp for air.

Onur slumped against the wall to catch his breath. "Wow, that was sad," he panted to himself. "I really need to start working out."

Realizing he wasn't about to move the fully outfitted guard anytime soon, he patted the man down until he found his keycard and retractable lanyard. He stood with the keycard in hand and approached the door, pulling slack line from the retractable device on the man's belt.

He reached out with the card as he attempted

to swipe it through the security panel, but his hand jerked to a stop a foot from the lock. He sighed heavily as he noticed he had pulled the taut lanyard to its maximum length. He would need to drag the guard a good foot closer to the door if he was going to be able to use the keycard without detaching it from the security guard's belt.

Onur slid down the wall and sat with his back propped up against the left side door. He planted both his feet against the unconscious man, pushing with his legs to move him. He huffed as he managed to successfully roll the man somewhat closer to the door.

He clambered to his feet and grabbed the keycard, swiping it through the security panel and enjoying the satisfying click as the door unlocked. He grabbed his phone, stepped through into the empty corridor and began making his way down another dimly lit hallway before a sudden realization hit him, forcing him to quickly turn and snatch at the handle to keep it from shutting.

I won't be able to open this again from this side if it shuts.

After a moment of thought he reached through the door crack and grabbed the guard's hand, letting the steel portal rest gently open against it.

"Thanks, buddy. You helped me out twice now."

He thanked the still very unconscious man as he proceeded down this second hallway. Stealing a glance at his phone, he hoped for some trace of the signal he was searching for but found none.

Dammit, I'm further inside but I still can't connect to him.

He walked a few feet down the hallway and breathed a sigh of relief as he spotted the door to a men's bathroom and ducked in. He headed directly into the last stall, locking it for privacy.

Another bit of luck I wasn't expecting.

As he crouched on the toilet to keep his feet hidden, he navigated the smartphone once again.

Come on, buddy. Please give me some good news.

Onur kept the phone moving as he waved it up high and around in the stall in hopes of improving his signal.

"Still can't establish connection?" he muttered angrily before reaching into his pocket, worried that perhaps they had captured his small robotic friend.

He took out a small pronged component and clicked it into the bottom of his phone.

If at first you don't succeed, boost the hell out of the signal.

He knew this would drain his battery, so he worked fast, pressing scan once again. The screen switched over to a live camera feed somewhere in the building's ducts and Onur clamped his mouth shut when he nearly cried out in triumph.

"Did you find him?" he whispered urgently into the phone, knowing that what scant amount of time he had bought himself was running out.

<Yes> flared the response on the screen, giving him the first real hope he'd felt since he had stepped foot in the warehouse.

"Good, Alton. Get near him and turn your microphone on, and hurry," he commanded into the phone, watching the small robot's progress through his screen.

His robotic creation moved from deeper in the duct towards the vent slits, peering down through the gaps at the bound man covered in bruises and blood.

Alton slipped through the grate and flew down to the man until it rested on his shoulder.

*

Jim could hear the ocean waves rumble against the coast as he watched his tiny daughter run up and down the beach, but never too far. Orange and fiery red light played alongside her as the sun set into the ocean.

I remember when she was so little . . .

He turned up the way to see his wife walking towards him with her sandals in hand.

She loves to feel the sand between her toes.

An annoying buzz sounded near his ear; Jim's first thought was a mosquito. He tried to reach up and swat it away, but realized his hands would not move.

The beach disappeared, his family replaced by darkness as he felt the bindings cutting into his wrists.

He woke with a start as the warehouse room came back into focus, jerking in sudden surprise at the small metal creature on his shoulder.

"Onur?"

"If you had to ask, Jim, then I can't be surprised you never caught me. Who else do you know in Fenny who builds advanced AI robots?"

Jim grinned then grimaced as his split lip reopened, a trickle of blood running down his mouth.

"Geez, Jim, they really worked you over." Onur spoke softly, surprising him with a tone of sympathy.

Hearing the emotion in Onur's voice was just as surprising to Jim, but not because he thought Onur wouldn't care.

The secretive hacker just wasn't one to show how he felt.

Definitely not like him, Jim thought.

"I must look worse than I feel if I'm getting some motherly love from you," he said.

Onur laughed.

"I dont know about motherly," Onur responded thoughtfully as he pondered a comparison.

"Maybe, like, an aunt you only see when she breaks up with one of her boyfriends and comes to your mom for support? She kinda sees you there and knows she has to say something, but she really just wants to cry to your mom?"

"That's . . . sweet?" Jim questioned sarcastically, their banter the same as always.

Onur had been one of those cases that had been dumped into Jim's lap on his first day as Chief of Police. A brilliant hacker that had been living and operating in Fenicia for years, he was infuriatingly difficult to even identify, let alone catch. It was a lesson Jim had learned the difficult way during his first year in charge.

With the FPD cybercrime division unable to gather so much as an age or real name let alone actual description, Onur had remained three steps ahead of the FPD at every turn. During that first year Jim had brought the hammer of the force down in an attempt to catch him, later admitting publicly that it had been a complete waste of police resources.

With pressing needs from the city on every side Jim was eventually forced to issue the order that if you somehow stumbled across the hacker arrest him, but don't waste time chasing him. Considering that Onur's crimes consisted almost entirely of credit card fraud unless provoked, it was an easy decision to focus on the vicious crime actually happening on the streets.

But when provoked, the kid had a blast routinely embarrassing Jim's tech and cybercrime department, leaving them utterly baffled at his abilities. Once he even went so far as to modify the department computers so that every keystroke and click of a mouse played a series of oinks and pig squeals.

But with Herod tightening his grip on the city, Jim remembered how they both had realized that working together was better than any alternative Herod would offer for either of them.

"Nah, sweet would be able to see the look on Herod's face at the exact moment he walks in and sees you missing, now come on, let's get those bindings loose," Onur spoke hurriedly.

Jim shook his head no, his lips forming a small smile as he tried to find the words he knew Onur wouldn't want to hear.

"Onur . . ." Jim began softly, "As much as I'm touched, and damn surprised that you made it to me, you need to . . ." was all he managed before being angrily interrupted.

"Get us the hell out of here? Yeah, working on it, Jim." The hacker said curtly, "Alton, get to work on cutting those bindings," he commanded, the small robot on Jim's shoulder immediately buzzing to attention and flitting onto the thick bindings holding the large man restrained.

"Onur," Jim said again in an attempt to get his attention.

Onur ignored Jim and continued working his phone.

Fed up with being ignored Jim raised his voice, bellowing "ONUR" loudly.

"What?" He finally responded in an annoyed tone.

Jim took a deep breath.

"Listen, if he didn't know you were here before he definitely knows now."

Onur snickered.

"No, he definitely knew I was here before. But thanks to my little buddy who is currently cutting your bindings, all the security cameras are being fed a loop."

Truly impressed with the kid but still seeing no hope in getting himself out of this building, Jim sighed.

"You have to get out of here, there is no way in hell you're getting me out and you know it. Unless this tiny bug can carry me, I can't walk."

*

Onur gritted his teeth as helplessness infuriated him. "Jim, you gotta know that if I leave now and I don't have you with me . . . Fenny doesn't stand a chance, man."

The bound man remained quiet as a few moments passed between them.

"Listen, kid, I don't have any answers, I really don't," Jim admitted quietly, "but I can tell you I don't believe that. You know why? Because there are people like you out there."

"Person, you mean? As in the singular? As in just me?"

"Trust me, I have a feeling," he said before becoming somber and quiet.

Onur felt a distinct sinking feeling in his stomach as he realized what Jim was about to ask.

"Did . . . did he get them?" Jim questioned tentatively.

Onur squeezed his eyes shut and stayed quiet, having no idea of how to possibly tell the already broken man. Silence seemed to be all the answer Jim needed, a few seconds passing before Onur could hear his deep sobs.

Sitting in his stall awkwardly he listened to the man cry, not knowing what to do but unwilling to leave him alone. He knew there was nothing he could do, not with security getting closer and closer to pinpointing him.

Throughout his life he had always found that he could use his intelligence and grasp of technology to gain what he wanted from whomever he wanted. But the recent months spent waging a losing war with Herod had left him feeling more useless than he had ever felt in his entire life.

Onur's throat tightened, tears stinging his eyes as he listened to the heartfelt sobs of fear and worry Jim shed for his wife and daughter.

In anger and frustration, Onur punched the stall wall, only succeeding in splitting the skin over two knuckles and bruising the rest.

"Fuck!" he softly screamed in pain as his fist throbbed.

Usually pragmatic, he was not one prone to useless emotional outbursts, leaving him genuinely surprised at his behavior.

Maybe you just never really cared about anyone before.

"Onur." Jim unexpectedly broke the silence with a voice now more conviction than sadness.

Surprised at the change in the man, Onur responded through clenched teeth as he held his bloody and painful hand.

"Yesshh?"

"I don't ask this lightly, and I know we have a history, and it's completely unfair to ask this of you . . . but you're the only person I think can help . . ." Jim started, speaking slowly but purposefully.

"I already was, big guy, I already was," Onur finished determinedly.

"Thank you. At least someone is trying to help my family."

Onur sat alone in the bathroom stall before hearing the approach of two men talking, his heart nearly jumping out of his chest in panic.

"Seriously, it was a bang from that bathroom and this whole friggin' dock is closed, swear to God," he heard the one say.

"Yeah, yeah," came the other man's reply, "Another one of your ghost stories, huh?"

The two voices moved closer as Onur's mind sifted through possibilities for escape.

His plans, however, inevitably hit the snag of being in a small bathroom with only one exit. An exit soon to be crowded by two armed men.

"Jim, I have company . . ." He whispered into the phone, letting it go at that.

"Get Out NOW," Jim growled, wasting no time in demanding Onur leave.

"Alton, find a line for the power control system!" Onur whispered urgently to the small robot.

"And when I hit the pound key cut power to this bathroom, trip the fire alarm, and then GET OUT."

As soon as Alton performed any override to the main

system, security would have a very good idea of where the small robot was hiding.

The two guards eased the bathroom door open as they remained quiet, listening for any sounds.

Despite their attempts at quiet, Onur could hear their thick boots squeaking on the tiled floor as they began making their way down the line of stalls, each door creaking open as they checked for occupants. Onur recalled the number of stalls in the bathroom as he made a mental note of how far they were from his.

That's three stalls away from mine. Time to gtfo.

Quietly sliding off of the toilet, he hit the pound key on the phone.

Almost immediately the bathroom became pitch black as the power to the lights switched off and the single fire alarm in the room began to blare.

"What is going on?" yelled one of the guards as he clapped his hands to his ears, the other trying to yell over the din as well.

"I told you something was going on!"

Using the darkness and distraction, Onur slid onto his stomach and slithered under the neighboring walls of bathroom stalls, quietly making his way towards the bathroom exit.

He bit his tongue as his hand hit a small puddle near the base of a toilet.

Oh, please be condensation, he begged as he continued crawling towards the exit.

As he reached the last stall, he crawled past it, raising himself into a crouch next to the bathroom's door as he heard the two men fumbling in pockets and gear belts for their flashlights. Before either man could turn their equipment on, light flooded the bathroom again as the system restored power, the bright lights forcing them to blink and reorient.

Onur wasted no time in running down the corridor the way he had come, slipping past the security door that remained propped open by the unconscious guard's hand. He sprinted out of the warehouse and to the chain link perimeter fence, ducking through the large gash he had cut earlier.

Onur ran flat out for a few minutes before his legs demanded a break, chest heaving as he tried to catch his breath.

"God dammit!" he screamed hoarsely into the night, fists clenched in an anger that was slowly dissipating into exhaustion. Shoulders slumped with the weight of Jim's daughter and wife, he slowly made his way along the shoreline towards the bright city lights of Fenicia, his mind a racing blur of thoughts and fears.

He listened to the soft lap of the waves against the shore and sighed.

“I have never needed a drink as bad as I do now,” he muttered into the night.

Not trusting in fate or chance to provide a drunken night he altered his course, ensuring that he did indeed pass a liquor store on the way home.

CHAPTER 6

Soft beams of early morning sunlight streamed into the bedroom, the thin rays playing with small floating bits of dust. Cold air and morning mist from the woods seeped in through the open window.

Nius's breathing was slow and steady as he sat slumped in the wooden chair, asleep, cheek pressed against the book of ancient religions that had kept him awake until the early morning hours. The sun continued its climb in the cool morning, and bright rays of sunlight began to uncomfortably illuminate his face and prick his eyelids, rousing him from sleep.

Nius lifted his head groggily and scanned his surroundings for anything out of the ordinary, double-checking where he was after last night's surprise at the bottom of a lake.

"At least I'm still in my room," he muttered, bringing

hands up to his face and attempting to rub the drowsiness out of his eyes.

Nius stood, reaching up towards the ceiling on tiptoes in a much-needed stretch, and then collapsed onto his bed. The clinking of plates and glasses from downstairs indicated Cheryl was up and about. His stomach growled at the thought of breakfast.

With this new incentive, he managed to drag himself sideways out of bed and to his door. The smell of fried eggs and bacon greeted him as he opened it. He made his way down the stairs and turned the corner into the dining area where Cheryl was already setting his place.

Nius had kept his late-night swim a secret from Cheryl, justifying the decision to keep her in the dark by telling himself it was to keep her from worrying.

An excuse that rang hollow even to him.

"Nice to see you using the steps this time," Cheryl quipped.

"Really? I don't even get a break for breakfast?" Nius groaned. He had woken her while returning from the lake, barging in through his window before tangling himself in a heap with the rug at the bottom of the staircase. He had explained it away as a late-night swing through the forest, but he knew she would now relish any opportunity to tease him about it.

While Cheryl was aware of his habit of climbing and jumping from tree to tree, she had made it clear she was less than enthusiastic about the whole thing.

"Speaking of a break, did you manage to fix your door after barreling through it?"

"Come on already!"

"Well, quit lobbing perfect set ups and I won't hit home runs!" she said with a deep laugh, letting him eat his breakfast in peace as she settled in to eat as well.

"So what are you thinking of doing today, aside from fixing your door so it locks again?"

"I was hoping to go into town for a bit. I think my book arrived yesterday and I wanted to check the P.O. box."

He watched Cheryl's face twitch a bit.

She nodded, chewing thoughtfully before answering. "That's, fine Nius, and I know you're sick of hearing me say it . . ."

Nius nodded with a mouth full of bacon and eggs. "Dun leh anyun shee me do shuff," he attempted before he gave up and stopped to swallow.

Cheryl rolled her eyes. "You realize Mona would have beat you senseless if she heard you talking with your mouth full, right?"

Nius nodded sheepishly, agreeing with his smirk.

*

Cheryl watched Nius devour his breakfast. In truth, she wasn't at all upset about him venturing into town more often. Finding a romance or at the very least some friends seemed like a great idea to her.

After so many years here, the locals were turning out to be much kinder than she had given them credit for. Especially after they learned of Mona's passing. While not many in the small community had agreed with a two-woman couple, a good portion of them were not hateful people. The pain of a lost loved one was universal as far as they were concerned.

Mona had been the one to make the decision to hide Nius away, for fear of what he could unknowingly do in public. It had been an understandable fear, Cheryl agreed. As an infant the extent of his abilities was a mystery, along with his control of them.

Recently, Cheryl had begun to wonder if the coldness or dislike they thought they had felt from the locals was more in response to Mona's standoffish behavior towards them. But she could never blame the woman for her protective actions. For all she knew, they were the reason Nius had grown up away from prying eyes.

But as the boy grew older and matured, just like any other child, she realized with a heavy heart that it was possible they had been overprotective. Maybe even downright restrictive with him.

Who am I to second-guess her? she pondered while munching a piece of bacon. *I mean, he is safe; no one bothers us. I wish you could see him, my love. He grew up to be such an amazing kid. You would be so proud.*

Cheryl recalled a sweet memory of Mona and her habit of mouthing "I love you."

"Want a ride into town?" Cheryl asked.

"No—I . . . I'll walk," he answered.

Cheryl sighed heavily. Nius was obviously planning to do very little walking, but she said

nothing else. After all, as long as he promised to remain unseen, there really was no danger to his tree hopping.

"So what had you so engrossed and up reading late last night?" Cheryl asked, nudging the conversation towards what she hoped would be a more pleasant direction.

He looked up with his eyes flashing excitedly. He'd always loved ancient histories and religions and lore. It showed as his face beamed in excitement, a childish grin widening that matched his tone.

"It's an entire book written on the angels in the Christian Bible, and how they appear and the amazing things they were said to have done. There was even one story about how a single angel of God killed nearly 200,000 men in a few hours."

"Wow, any particular reason why all those men had to die?"

"Well, he didn't kill them all . . ."

"Oh, good. Just most of them, right?" she teased.

"You get so used to thinking that right and wrong is always black and white. You don't think about the gray areas and it gets confusing."

"That is one of the wisest things I have ever heard you say, Nius. I'm proud of you. It's the people who have decided that there are no gray areas when it comes to right and wrong that scare me. Life is too complicated to be so neatly categorized in my opinion."

Nius looked around at the simple home and furnishings. "Our lives don't seem so complicated."

She smiled from behind her coffee cup. "I'm half of a lesbian couple living in the woods who found a kid in the blown-to-bits ruins of an abandoned shop in the city. An infant, mind you, who seems incapable of getting sick or hurt."

With a grin, he conceded her point.

Cheryl sighed wistfully, setting down her cup. "Trust me, even those out there who live their lives free of the supernatural still face difficult decisions with no easy answers.

Picking up her cup she took a long drink of the now lukewarm coffee, unwilling to waste it. "But enough about that, what about your future? Just two more years until you're eighteen, given any thought about what you want to do? Where do you want to go?"

*

The first two times Cheryl had asked him about what he wanted in life, he was surprised and the prospect had left him thinking for days. With his K-12 education completed through a correspondence school, he could go to college with his grades and test scores. While the thought of campus life and meeting so many new people and friends was both terrifying and exciting to Nius, he knew what Mona would have said and his shoulders slumped.

"I am meant for so much more," he whispered under his breath.

"I suppose I can stick around here for a bit?" he said with a slight shrug that communicated his feelings about the prospect.

"No thoughts on college? You wouldn't stop talking about campuses just a few months ago."

"It's just that it's so expensive . . ."

"Don't give me that. You know I have a college fund saved for you, and the rest we can do with loans."

He shook his head, wanting to be done with the conversation.

"So you want to stay here and do what? Read books and swing around trees? Avoid people at all cost for the rest of your life?"

There was a harshness in her voice that surprised him.

"If this is about Mona and what she wanted for you I would like to remind you that apathy and agoraphobia were not in her plans. You sit here and sulk watching a girl you clearly adore skip away without so much as a conversation."

Cheryl leaned back in her chair as she crossed her arms in front of her. "If Mona was so worried about you being some sort of savior for this world, then I'm sure you shouldn't be hiding from said world."

He felt as though she had slapped him.

"What exactly are you trying to protect me from, Nius? From being involved in your life? From knowing you? From loving you? Don't you understand that if you try to save me by detaching yourself, by cutting me away from your life, you have protected nothing?"

Nius could find no words that countered the sting of the truth in hers. A lot more made sense to the youth, another realization of just how little he understood and how much he had to learn.

The silence stretched as Cheryl rose from her seat and walked over to the stove. She poured more coffee into the now cool cup.

Nius fidgeted in his chair before he spoke. “I think I need to find out what I am. Why I’m here. I think I need to go to Fenicia where you found me.”

It was Cheryl’s turn to be taken by surprise. “I knew you wanted to understand where you come from, but I had no idea it had already crystallized into any sort of a plan. But I understand, Nius, and I think that is what you should do, if that is what you want to do.”

He nodded slowly in agreement as the logistics and reality of the conversation hit him like an ocean liner gradually beaching itself.

How was he going to get there? Where would he start when he got there? Most importantly, what exactly was he looking for?

Almost as if she could hear the questions that now occupied his thoughts, Cheryl rose from her chair and walked to a small desk near the front door of the cabin. Ripping a small page from the memo pad they used to leave notes for each other, she wrote a few words before returning to the table and pushing the small paper towards him.

“I think your best bet is to start here.”

Nius looked down at the slip of paper and recognized

it as an address in the huge city hundreds of miles away. "What is it?"

"The location of the pawn shop we found you in. Of course, when we found you, it was more of a smoking hole in the ground. If there are any answers for you to find in Fenny, I imagine they might start there."

Nius stared at the address scribbled on the slip of paper. His scattered thoughts careened around in his head as he tried to think. Though he had begun tentative planning weeks ago, it was still a terrifying prospect, and admitting his plan to Cheryl had made it more real, more concrete, and more worrisome.

"I can even take out some money for you to get started in Fenny. I'm not that worried about you being safe, but you still need somewhere to live and food to eat. I'm sure we can take out at least $10,000 from the savings for you."

"What? I don't need all that." He balked at the amount, more money than he could really even imagine.

Cheryl waved away his doubts with a flourish as she seemed to grow more and more excited while planning for him. She headed for her office.

"You don't understand the city, hun. It's very expensive living."

He remained quiet and Cheryl stopped before settling into the empty seat nearest him. "Listen, you know you will always be welcome here and this place will always be your

home. But as a home, Nius. Not some sort of self-imposed prison from where you watch your life pass you by."

"I have a question for you."

"Anything." Cheryl promised sincerely, and he knew she meant it.

"If I had said I wanted to go to college first, would you still have given me $10,000 cash?" He grinned.

Cheryl burst into laughter and Nius joined her.

"Yes! You would already be out and I would have had your bags packed ages ago!"

They shared the laugh before it died away.

Cheryl reached over and moved his hair from his eyes. "You may not get sick or hurt Nius, but from what we can tell, you're still bound to time and I was getting sick of watching you waste the precious little we are all given."

Nius nodded in agreement before leaning over and giving her a tight squeeze.

"Thank you," he whispered.

"You are very welcome. Now go. Get out of here and go check on your book or see Lauren. I have a lot of planning to do."

Nius slipped his feet into his shoes and headed out

the door towards town feeling less burdened than when he had awoken that morning.

*

Stepping on the twigs and dry leaves that carpeted the forest floor he crunched along, working on putting distance between himself and the cabin. He took a deep breath of the sweet pine scent from the large trees and closed his eyes for a few steps, enjoying the crisp clean air.

Nius watched and listened to the forest bustle with activity. Squirrels skittered above him leaping from branch to branch as they played in the balmy winter weather, exchanging their usual search for food with some levity. Beautiful warbling flooded the deep woods punctuated by sharp chirps as the song birds called to each other, their warnings and welcomes unknown to casual observers.

Nius smiled in satisfaction as his heart swelled with joy. He was always taken with the natural world of the deep woods that he loved. Behind him the light gray sky soon filled with treetops as he left the cabin behind.

"That should be far enough away to not give Cheryl a heart attack." He chuckled, eying the tree branches above him and searching for a good opening.

He spotted what he was looking for and sprinted

with incredible speed towards the tree before running up the trunk a few steps. He grabbed the branch above him while kicking off the trunk with his foot, swinging up and onto the tree limb before slowly standing up. With perfect balance he stood on the branch and looked around.

Nius took off sprinting along the thin branch towards the trunk and repeated the same maneuver as he made his way towards its peak.

As he reached the top of the tree, he scanned the forest, searching for signs of anyone else from the much higher vantage point. With the woods appearing empty of anyone for miles, he began to rock back and forth in the tree forcing it to bend and swing with his weight.

Nius clutched the top as the entire thing swayed wildly and readied himself to jump, the pine bending before violently snapping back in the opposite direction.

The woods beneath him sped past in a blur as he slingshotted through the air.

He bit back a euphoric yell and went spinning like a football through the sky. The freedom was exhilarating as he whipped through the forest like a missile.

He sensed a large tree speeding towards him and turned so he was backwards. Neighboring pine branches slapped his back as he rocketed past. He reached up and grabbed a thick branch above, his momentum swinging himself up into the sky above the canopy. With arms outstretched towards the brilliant sun he aimed his face towards the heavens.

His ascent towards the clouds slowed as gravity began tugging him back towards earth, the odd drop in his gut warning him that he had begun to fall.

He'd planned to swing again from a branch as the trees hurtled up towards him, but he faltered as a girl's laughter bounced around the thick underbrush below. In a panic, he reached out desperately and grabbed a much thinner branch than he intended. With a loud crack, the weak limb snapped and dropped Nius towards the hard ground.

He plummeted like a rock before slowing inches from the earth. His feet touched down lightly as Lauren stepped out from the thick growth.

Her long blonde hair was woven into a beautiful braid and she wore a wool sweater covered by a camo jacket and jeans. Snow boots were pulled up to her calves as she walked the woods. Lauren smiled as she waved to Nius. Her boisterous cream-and-black puppy Bruno leapt about, yipping and licking at both of them in joy.

Nius returned the smile and racked his brain for something clever or funny to say, but the broken branch finished following him down and hit him squarely in the head.

Lauren's eyes widened in worry. "Are you ok?"

Though it had not actually hurt him, Nius rubbed the back of his head and hoped the embarrassing moment would just pass so his cheeks would stop burning pink.

"Yeah, I'm fine," he replied nonchalantly.

Lauren looked up into the tree to spot where the branch had fallen from. "That is so weird that it just fell like that. I mean, Bruno gets the squirrels so mad that I see them throw nuts and twigs down at him but I have never seen them throw an entire branch," she joked.

"Yeah, I told them walnuts taste terrible and almonds are better." he replied.

The sound of her laughter had a detrimental effect on his ability to think straight.

"Were you headed to town? Bru and I were going there ourselves. Let's group up."

Her hopeful tone put Nius more at ease.

"Bru can take the squirrel hate from here on out."

They walked side by side with the puppy between them. Quiet settled over the conversation and Nius began to worry that maybe he was coming off as boring.

"So how is—"

"How is everyone—"

They started at the same time and stopped before Nius plowed forward.

"How is everyone at the house?" he asked.

"Good. Season is starting up and hunters are flooding into town. Dad and Will are excited about some big bucks they keep spotting. I'm heading over to see the new gear those out-of-towners are bringing."

His stomach dropped at the mention of hunting season.

Killing things with rifles didn't exactly appeal to him but he had learned not to mention it to anyone else. A town this deep in the forest was practically required to celebrate the annual hunting season. The much-needed revenue from the visiting hunters was a welcome addition and folks were generally not happy about anyone with differing opinions.

Nius argued with himself as his hand began to reach for Laurens's, but he lost courage.

Come on, man, just hold her hand.

He faltered again as his pep talked failed.

Nius thought once more to grab her hand but was surprised as hers took hold of his instead and squeezed it. Looking from her hand to the warm look on her face he felt as if his heart might melt.

They walked a few more steps holding hands before a loud guffaw sounded from the woods in front of them. The laughing was followed by jeers and yells of other boys nearby.

Nius slowed as he heard the sounds until he found

himself being tugged by Lauren to keep him moving and following.

"No, no more of this. This is stupid and we all live together in the town and this is ridiculous."

"I don't care, but you know *they* can't help it."

"I don't give up that easily, Nius. This is the fastest way to town."

With renewed effort she tugged his arm until they both were keeping pace. As they approached, the noise died down.

Breaking into the clearing, Nius and Lauren looked over at where the four teenagers sat in the back of a pickup truck. The guys were drinking light beers and were clearly already a few in. Their hunting rifles leaned against the vehicle.

"Hey, look. Lauren's walking her weirdo!" one yelled as the rest brayed.

"Shut it, Jon," Lauren shot back as she narrowed her eyes at the rifles.

Jon's cheeks flushed with anger as he eyed their handholding. His own previous relationship with Lauren was a well-known fact around town.

"You know those shouldn't be loaded, right? And you definitely shouldn't be drinking with them loaded."

Jon stepped off the truck bed and grabbed his rifle.

He rested the barrel on his shoulder as he downed the remains of the beer he had been drinking.

"Nag nag nag, you know you aren't pretty enough for a guy to put up with that mouth."

Lauren smiled. "Nius doesn't mind, do you?"

"Uh . . . yeah," Nius said at a loss as to how to respond.

"M'yeah," Jon said in a mocking voice while walking over to the two as his friends remained in the truck watching and grinning.

"What are you doing with Lauren, loser?"

Nius was used to the treatment and tried to remain friendly and neutral.

The friendliness only seemed to infuriate Jon further.

Jon glared at Nius as he bounced the rifle on his shoulder before bringing it down, pointing the barrel but with his finger off the trigger.

The two jerked back away from the weapon in fear before Nius pushed Lauren away from himself and the loaded weapon's aim.

"Oh ho, isn't that sweet, guys?" Jon mocked, waving the rifle around Nius for emphasis.

"Can you please stop swinging a loaded rifle around, Jon?" Lauren's voice was low and scared.

"Why? What do you have to worry about with this loser faggot protecting you? How does it work being raised by lesbos? You turn out a fag or do you just want a vag?"

Jon moved and shoved Nius as the boys in the truck jeered, but Nius didn't move an inch. The shove instead pushed Jon backwards as if he had pushed against a building.

Not understanding what had just happened, Jon peered at the strange kid. Voices from the truck were now hushed. Jon tossed his rifle aside as he clenched fists and stepped towards Nius.

The thrown gun fired wildly towards Nius with a boom that left ears ringing.

"Did you see that shit? The fucking air in front of the weirdo glowed!" one of the boys from the truck yelled in the stillness after the misfire.

Nius cared little and turned instead to Lauren.

"Are you all ri—"

The words died on his lips as his heart dropped into his stomach. Her skin was as pale as paper as her eyes unfocused. Blood streamed freely between the fingers of her hand as she clutched at her collarbone.

Her eyes rolled and disappeared into her skull as she fell to her knees. Nius moved quickly and caught her, lowering her to the ground.

"Lauren? Lauren?" he called in desperation, trying to get her to respond.

Reaching for her collarbone he desperately hoped that something he could do would help stem the bleeding.

Without warning his breath left him, a small surge in his fingertips weakening him.

A loud click sounded from behind Nius as Jon cocked the rifle. He could almost feel the barrel against his head.

"Get the fuck away from her, you freak. I won't let you hurt her anymore," Jon growled.

The blood pouring from Lauren's shoulder had slowed but still ran freely and she remained unconscious. Nius felt cold unfamiliar panic and fear squeeze his chest tight, making his breaths shallow as he watched her bleeding in front of his eyes.

"Will someone call 911!" he screamed at them.

"GET AWAY FROM HER," Jon screamed back, his gun shaking in unsteady hands.

Nius put his hands up in surrender. He was terrified, but not for himself as he rose to his feet. He looked towards the truck and breathed a sigh of relief as two of the boys had their cellphones to their ears.

Jon tried to get close to Lauren but an angry and protective Bruno rushed up to him growling and barking in an attempt to protect the injured girl.

The dog yelped in pain as Jon's heavy kick launched the puppy away from her side.

Nius snatched the dog up in his arms before running off with him into the woods, desperately hoping that Lauren would be ok.

CHAPTER 7

January 3rd
Monday, Noon

The splatters and pools of drying blood from the night before created a morbid rainbow of reds and crimsons around the room, the dampness of the basement floor keeping the puddle surrounding Gene's corpse a bright hue. The soles of Herod's leather shoes clicked loudly against the concrete as he walked from Gene's body to the basement's mangled door-frame again, piecing together the story the location of the blood was trying to tell. He stepped with confidence, knowing his unbuttoned casual suit fit well on his toned body—knowing this intimidated those around him. Periodically, he glanced at the contents of a thin folder he otherwise kept wedged under his arm. Along the walls of the room stood a dozen Fenicia PD officers, watching while Herod and two detectives paced the room examining the gruesome scene.

Herod shook his head as he inspected the mangled door frame. Holding out his hand to indicate the destruction, he turned to the two detectives.

"Explain this to me, because I can see what happened. I just have trouble believing it." The two detectives looked at each other, unsure of what to say. "Judging by the position of the corpse and the hospital bed, it looks like . . . Well . . . it would have to . . ." The detective stammered to a silence, uncertain of how to continue. Everyone in the room could see what the evidence and scene told of the previous night's blood bath. Herod took a deep breath, exhaling through his nose like a bothered bull before taking a step towards the detective to encourage him to speak.

The officer sighed before hurrying through his speculations. "It would appear that whoever was bound to this hospital bed ripped the restraints loose, tore Father Gene's throat out, and proceeded to punch that steel security door free from its frame. But . . . I don't quite understand how that's possible. It would have to be someone impossibly strong."

"Let's just assume that's the case, then, shall we?" Herod gestured for the man to continue.

The detective cleared his throat. "There are no

security cameras down here, and the victim had called off his own house security for the night."

"Everything you just told me I already knew. I specifically asked you to explain it to me." Herod moved around the hospital bed, taking care to avoid the large pool of Gene's blood. "Who and how did they rip these restraints, who murdered Gene and why?" Herod knew full well the detectives had no answers he himself didn't already have. He allowed his rage to flare, raising his voice to a yell. "And most importantly, how in the hell did they punch through a steel door?"

The two men shrank away from his anger, joining their colleagues along the wall as Herod knelt by the hospital bed to examine the torn restraints. Excitement bordering on fury had begun to build in his chest, fingers shaking as they felt the thick warped steel of the bed frame. *Goddamn you, Gene, I told you to leave her be*, Herod thought angrily, and wondered where he could find her now. He had hoped for more information from such seasoned veterans of the force, but was disappointed. He knew it wasn't really their fault. He already knew more about the situation than they did, and they had just arrived. Still, he wanted to continue to feel his rage.

This is impossible, Herod thought, trembling in incensed excitement, his breathing quick as he pondered the possibilities. If this was all somehow real, Ann could represent what he so desperately needed. Dave's absolute unwillingness to part with her made much more sense to him now. *He must have known about you and figured you to be a goldmine*, Herod reasoned. It had not made any sense that Dave continued risking his life to protect the small orphan that wasn't his own kid.

Rising to his feet, he faced the detectives. "Have you located Dave?"

They shook their heads no, but one piped up. "But we *have* located his abandoned car in the downtown parking garage. Surveillance shows him and a girl leaving the vehicle and heading into the city."

Herod's face broke into a grin.

"We followed them on surveillance for a few blocks but we lost them near Kahve's Coffee."

She must be nearby, Herod reasoned, *but what of him?*

"I want Dave found," Herod announced, the men and women beginning to hurry out before he raised his palm to stop them. "But much more importantly, I want her found." He again pulled Gene's folder from under his arm. Taking out her placement center headshot, he held it up for all to see before giving it to a detective to circulate. Ever a meticulous man, Gene had kept files on all the potential future girls for his illegal brothels, though only Ann's was found in his bedroom—the rest he'd kept in his office.

"Consider her armed and dangerous, and do not approach her without back up," he commanded before pausing.

"If she is in any way hurt or killed, I will kill you," he stated before adding, "and everyone you love," as an afterthought before walking up the steps.

Reaching the floor level of the home, Herod entered the beautiful dining room. Gene's wooden table and handcrafted chairs had been shoved unceremoniously into a corner to make room for the team examining the steel security door that had secured the basement. One of the crew spotted Herod and signaled to the others to stand against the wall but Herod stopped them, waving for them to continue working. He leaned against the dining room wall as he stared at the mangled slab of metal, awed by the power it had seen. It had been a single strike, no evidence of any other impacts. No acids or chemicals, no gas torches, no explosions or discolorations. A single strike had ripped that steel slab from its frame, the evidence in the small, detailed fist indentation warped into the door.

The impact must have been incredible.

Vibrations from his pocket snapped his thoughts

back to the present. He pulled the cellphone out to see who was calling.

Norman? After trying to contact Gene's lackey all morning, Herod found it odd the man was now contacting him directly, considering their relationship. Though he was one of Herod's oldest employees, it was not really by choice.

"I don't suppose you know anything about what happened here at Gene's house, do you?" Herod skipped through any greeting.

"I heard he was dead." Norman revealed no semblance of emotion in his tone.

"Yeah, he is. Throat ripped out, and lots of other details that don't make sense. I'm hoping you can shed some light."

There was a long pause as Norman digested the news.

He has to be unsure of which direction to go now that Gene is dead.

Herod spoke up sensing the uncertainty. "I know Gene put a lot on your shoulders, Norm. I know he forced you to go behind my back and my anger lies with him, not you. He was your boss and you followed his orders."

"We need to talk," Norm replied.

"Isn't that what we are doing?" Herod bristled.

"I thought it wasn't safe to use cellphones. That there were people out there who might be list—"

"No, no, don't worry about that," Herod interrupted, knowing there were men on the way to the hacker's location at that very moment. "Jim's gone and whoever that kid was, I'm taking care of it."

Though more often an annoyance than a danger, there were few people in the world that Herod wanted shackled to a wall more than the clever hacker that had hounded and needled him these past few years. Herod was convinced he was responsible for the warehouse.

Norm remained quiet, not going any further over the phone.

"I really think we should talk in person."

Herod's curiosity was piqued as the pieces came together. *This isn't like Norman. He would probably prefer to never see me again, let alone insist on a meeting.*

"Fine. Stop by the penthouse for dinner," Herod answered. "And Norm? Keep him alive." The line cut out as, without another word, Norman hung up.

Tapping his phone against his leg, Herod pondered what else it could possibly be, but was unable to think of any other reasons for his behavior.

It has to be Dave. Gene must have left Norman to deal with him. Whatever it was, it was currently his only lead in the mess and Norman seemed almost desperate.

He sucked in a deep steadying breath and ran a hand through his dark hair. "I do not need this right now," he whispered. The pressures of the city and yesterday's events weighed heavily on his paranoid mind.

Though it had only been four short years since he had become the man behind the workings, running nearly every aspect of the city's government, the changes in the city were dramatic. Once considered a beautiful diamond on the coast, most of Fenicia's streets now lay pockmarked with holes, some in such disrepair they were impassable. A destination where people once sought the American dream now heaved with the homeless and unemployed. Jobs were nowhere to be found and help was nonexistent for the poor.

The wealthy in the city, however, prospered ever more under Herod's control after he slashed taxes on the rich to nearly nothing for political gain and personal cash flow, though this left the city scrambling to find the funds to function.

"Sir? Your car is out front."

His officers attended their tasks, avoiding eye contact as he walked past. Stepping out into the chill, he strode towards the beautiful black sedan idling under a sky gray and dark with rain. His driver stood beside the vehicle to open the passenger door for him.

"Take me to the penthouse," Herod demanded.

Once seated, he punched numbers into his cellphone dialing out.

"What can I do for you?" came a hushed voice.

"You must already know you're up, Fitz. You are in charge and I want the whole operation to continue running smoothly."

"I didn't know, but I'm glad to hear."

Herod could nearly hear the grin Fitzsimmons wore. The disgusting pervert made even Gene look like a saint.

"Do you have any leads?" Fitz asked tentatively.

"I know who. If I thought it was you, you would already be gone."

"Of course."

"One more thing. I plan on Jim's wife and daughter working for you soon, make sure you put them through orientation."

"It would be my deepest pleasure."

A light freezing rain tapped against the warm car as they drove in silence. Herod looked out the window and watched as the city center passed by. The sidewalks were packed with shoppers, pricey boutiques and coffee shops filled with patrons trying to escape the bout of freezing water. Droplets darkened the concrete before collecting in puddles or joining the small streams along the street, reflecting the beautiful colors of downtown Fenny's lights.

Had he been so inclined, a drive just twenty minutes in any direction would have revealed a much different and starker picture of the state of Fenicia. The homeless and jobless choked the streets and alleyways of the poorest areas. But not here, not in the beautiful downtown where Herod paid good money for law enforcement to keep such "trash" out. He watched as his apartment building rose in the distance, the dark-gray concrete making it appear as if an ancient black obelisk was being pushed forth from the rainy mist by Gods.

Peeling away from traffic, they slid into the reserved lane leading into a parking garage, swerving left and heading down onto Herod's personal garage floor.

The car pulled around one of the building's massive concrete pillar supports and came to a stop, headlights illuminating Norman and his car. Norman sat in the front seat of his station wagon holding his keys, door open with shoes flat on the concrete of the garage. He appeared disheveled, obviously having spent the night away from home and without sleep.

He looks fucking worse than Gene. Herod stepped out and walked over to Norm's car. "Well?"

Norm sat sullen, shaking his head wanting no conversation. "Just take him."

"If him is Dave then I need you to be a lot more talkative." Herod peered through the windows of the vehicle, seeing no one else in the car.

Keys in hand, Norman squeezed his thumb and

pressed the car remote; the vehicle beeped and the trunk opened to reveal a very awake and unbound Dave.

I thought Norm looked rough. "You kept him in the trunk all night? And people think *I'm* a monster," Herod muttered, shaking his head and waving Dave out of the trunk.

"Come on out of there. Sit in the backseat like a man." Herod offered Dave before looking back to his driver. "Get us some food. I missed breakfast today." The man nodded shortly and proceeded off to do Herod's bidding.

Dave remained unmoving and defiant in the trunk.

"Come on, sit, eat, drink, we have lots to talk about."

Dave didn't move.

"I recommend you cooperate. We only have a few questions about Ann."

Dave stared him in the eyes, unwavering and unafraid. "How in the hell would I know where she is if I have been locked in here all morning?" he asked, face a scowl. "And even if—"

"I did know, I wouldn't tell you." Herod finished Dave's sentence, mocking him.

"Don't worry about where she is. We took care of that," Herod whispered, making sure to emphasize the "we."

He watched as the impact of his lie unraveled Dave's

resolve, shoulders slumping as if someone had let the air out of a balloon.

"When it comes to Ann, I'm more interested in the how and why."

Dave shut his eyes and leaned his head back, unmoving and unresponsive.

I am not getting anywhere this way. "Take him up to the penthouse and lock him in the unused wine storage. I want security on him every second of every minute, understand?"

Norm nodded his understanding.

"It's good to have you back, Norm. Get yourself cleaned up in the apartment. We have a lot to talk about." Herod finished.

Pulling the man from the trunk, Norman walked him towards the elevator with his hand wrapped around the back of Dave's neck.

Flipping open his phone, he quick-dialed the driver. "Forget the food; his cooperation wasn't deserving."

CHAPTER 8

January 3rd
Monday Evening

Sheets of freezing rain beat against the windows of the bus as if trying to force their way in. The passengers exhaled cold mist and bundled themselves tightly. Wedged in the corner where his seat met the window, Nius rested his head against the cold glass, bored of watching the rural landscape blur past. As the bus jostled and swayed over a pothole, passengers grabbed at their seat edges to keep from sliding off. Grab bars and seat belts had been removed. Empty bolt holes in the metal walls and frayed fabric protruding from the seats reminded the passengers of the missing luxury.

How much longer? After having spent the better part of seven hours on the noisy vehicle, his patience was wearing thin with the loud metal box on wheels.

He remembered what an exciting prospect the city used to be. Now he just worried about his circumstances and Cheryl's fate.

Eyes closed and mind free to wander, Nius allowed his memory of the previous day to replay itself. With Lauren shot and her dog in tow, Nius had burst into the cabin, nearly shortening his mom's life by heart attack before he was able to explain what had happened. She had looked somber but resolved.

Cheryl had taken him by the shoulders and faced him toward her. "If it was only her shoulder and help was on the way, then we can afford to hope that she is going to be fine. I know that girl, and she won't tell them you did anything unless it's what happened. But they are going to have a truck full of boys who are going to tell them god knows what. Just being involved means they are going to start looking into you. You have to leave and it has to be now."

Nius had known she was right, realizing with a sadness that their future farewell was staring them down. After a quick goodbye, Nius had shoved a smattering of belongings into his backpack and with Cheryl's parting gift of $10,000 cash, he fled. He'd traveled fast and hard through the forest, swinging and leaping through the dense woods until morning found him near the bus station that would take him to Fenicia.

Nius peered out the bus window again, watching the towers of Fenny's skyline dominate the horizon. The massive buildings seemed to stretch into the sky for an eternity.

As the bus shuddered along the packed and writhing highway that pierced the outskirts of the city, Nius noticed the passing landscape change, turning into more dirty concrete, garbage, and rusted steel than anything else.

This doesn't seem right. Did I get on the wrong bus?

Pulling out the small scrap of folded paper from his pocket Nius opened it carefully and reread the handwritten address. No, it was the right one.

The bus passed dark and shuttered storefronts with rundown people milling about outside. What few layers of clothing they owned were pulled close. The scene was nothing like the beautiful city Cheryl had always talked lovingly about. Nius looked around the bus in disbelief at the dead eyes and apathy of his fellow passengers. A small group in the entrance of an alley caught his eye. Nius noticed with alarm that two small children were among them.

The kids shook but whether with fear or anger, Nius didn't know. They were shouting at two uniformed officers who were beating an older man on the sidewalk. With tear-streaked red faces, the children looked like they wanted to run but were unwilling to abandon the man.

"Stop the bus!" he shouted. Grabbing his bag he leapt to his feet.

The bus roared on in an odd silence, no one acknowledging him. Nius stood up in the small aisle looking around, not knowing how to process being so ignored.

"Could . . . could you *please* stop the bus?" he asked politely but loud enough to be heard in case that had been the problem in the first place. The bus lurched and shook on while his second request faded away like the first.

Nius made his way to the front of the bus. The driver tensed and his left arm shifted to his side.

A few feet away from the thick yellow line sprayed onto the black rubber mat, Nius stopped and raised his hands.

"You're not going to stop the bus, are you?"

The older man shook his head. His eyes did not leave the road as his left arm shifted and rested on his lap, hand obviously clutching a weapon. "I stop the bus where I'm not supposed to, and a bunch of fellas jump on and beat me to death and rob you all. You want that?"

Nius studied the bus as he weighed his options.

"Fine."

Swinging his backpack on and tightening the straps,

Nius turned away from the front of the bus before sprinting down the tiny aisle towards the back. At the last second, he spun forward into a tight ball before kicking his feet through the back window and launching himself out.

Nius landed on the wet asphalt and watched as the bus sped on without him. He felt in his pocket for the scrap of paper containing Cheryl's scrawled note. He squeezed it in his palm and stared in the direction he should be heading. He turned his back and bolted in the direction of the kids he had seen.

Defunct parking meters blurred by as Nius sprinted extraordinarily fast, covering the mile-long distance in a few moments.

Spotting the police officers still torturing the helpless man, he switched to a light jog and crept forward as quietly as he could. He hoped to catch some clue about what was happening. Was the man possibly a criminal? A kidnapper caught red handed with children?

None of those felt right to Nius. Everything about the scene felt wrong.

"Please, please just don't kill our dad," the boy begged, unable to suck in a full breath through his tears.

As if in answer, one officer pulled back his leg. Nius watched his boot connect with the father's nose, creating an audible wet snap that infuriated Nius. The man wasn't resisting. He was barely conscious and yet the cops continued beating him as the man's kids watched and sobbed.

"Hey!" Nius surprised himself with how angry his voice sounded and the officers' heads jerked toward him.

"What do you want?" The shorter officer snarled. He took a few steps toward Nius but kept some distance.

Sliding his backpack off and dropping it, Nius stopped. He had their full attention now.

With the cops occupied, the two kids wasted no time in rushing to their father's side, pulling and dragging on the injured man as hard they could in an attempt to get him away.

"What's going on here? Do you guys need some help?" Nius asked.

The taller officer chuckled and slid his dense steel baton free of its holster.

"Tell you what, kid. I'll give you a chance to get outta here now before I knock all your teeth out." He slapped the baton in his open palm and took a step towards Nius.

Nius kept his eyes focused on the men and away from the kids as they continued trying to get their father on his feet.

"My teeth? That doesn't sound legal . . ."

The officer that had chuckled looked back at the two

kids and realized they were being distracted. Spinning, he swung with his baton and struck the small boy across the shoulder blades, drawing a pained scream from the child.

The cop readied the baton for another blow when a sudden strike to the back of his knee stopped him. His leg buckled and he was brought down to his knees.

Nius stared down the kneeling officer as the other man's baton slammed into the side of his head. Instead of the crack of skull the officers no doubt expected, there was a loud and sharp report that echoed off of the surrounding brick walls. The shorter officer dropped the metal stick as he grunted in pain and rubbed his hands furiously.

"It feels like I hit a steel post," he cried.

Nius didn't give them even a moment to regroup and punched the prostrate man squarely in the face. The thug went down moaning before even meeting the dirty concrete. Nius spun with his other fist outstretched and knocked the other officer free from his consciousness.

With his heart pounding against his chest, Nius felt his anger dissipating. It left behind only the bitter realization of having attacked uniformed police officers to worry about.

Nius raced to the injured boy who lay with his arm wrapped around his father's leg for comfort. His younger sister stood next to them, pink-faced and red-eyed from crying. Nius helped the boy up and gently rubbed his back trying to dissipate the pain of the injury, as he had seen Mona do on occasion for others. The kid cried out in pain and Nius retracted his hand.

"I'm so sorry. I was just trying to help. You ok?"

The boy nodded and grasped his sister's hand, pulling her close.

"What was that about? Why were the police being so cruel?" Nius asked. The skittish girl looked as though she might bolt if he took another step. Nius looked over the bloodied father, unsure he was still alive until spotting the chest rise and fall slightly.

If we don't get him help, he's gone.

"Listen, we need to get you all to a hospital."

At this, the nearly unconscious man spoke up. "Kid, you need to go. You need to run, and you need to hide. Just get away from here. If they find you, you're dead." He nodded toward the downed officers.

"What in the hell was that and who are you? Were they really cops? What did you do?" Nius blurted out unable to help himself.

"Those cops saw a struggling dad with two kids and did some math. They assumed I must have some money to take care of them." He paused, wincing and then spit blood onto the concrete. "Guess it was kind of my fault. I could have just taken a few punches, let them have their fun and walked away. But they threatened to take my kids . . . I lost it."

"Must be a new definition of the words 'my fault'," Nius muttered, looking around the depressing streets and wondering what had happened to the place Cheryl left behind.

"This is your first time in the outskirts, kid?"

Nius nodded but left it at that. "Listen, where do I take you? There are still hospitals, right?"

"Yeah, but none I can afford. You already helped us out. We can take it from here."

Nius leveled a look at the father and repeated the question with emphasis. "Where do I take you?"

"All right then. If you won't accept no for an answer." When he struggled to rise, Nius put out his hand to help him up. "I'm Adrian, kid."

"Nius."

Adrian nodded in the direction Nius had come from. "Down two blocks and then a right, there's a church. It's run by a guy named Terry. Good guy, medic in the war before becoming a priest. Seems a little backwards to me—seeing war then deciding you're sure there is a God, but that's him."

"You ok to walk?" Nius asked the boy. The kid

looked up at him making eye contact for the first time and nodded yes.

They reached the empty intersection and crossed before turning the corner. Nius spotted the small, unimpressive building that must have been Terry's church. He stared in surprise. There were no beautiful stained-glass motifs, no vaulted arches or intricate pillars. The simple square building's dank red bricks were held together by grimy lines of old mortar. Planted firmly in the tiny strip of lawn in front of the building stood a white cross with a dove etched into the painted wood. Horizontally along the crossbeam was the word Faith, and Hope was painted vertically down the post.

"That it?" Nius asked. His surprise drew a pained grin from Adrian.

"Yeah. I guess it's nothing like Father Gene's megachurch," Adrian agreed as he looked the old building over. "That one is nearly as big as the mall downtown."

Not knowing anything about any of this, Nius stayed quiet.

Once they reached the steps of the church, the doors burst open. The large man who emerged moved with grace, taking the steps three at a time. He wore black clerical pants and matching shirt with collar. Nius decided this must be Terry. Whatever physical training he had embraced during military service had clearly not been abandoned.

"Adrian? Graham, Steph, are you ok?" Terry pulled the two kids into a quick embrace before turning to their much worse-off father and Nius.

"Thank you for helping him."

The priest turned back to Adrian. "You stubborn donkey. I told you to stay here with the kids," Terry chided. He lifted the beaten man easily into his arms and carried Adrian up the steps. "A stubborn and rebellious generation; a generation that set not their heart aright, and whose spirit was not steadfast with God."

"Psalms 78, verse 8," Nius recalled aloud without thinking.

The priest stopped in his tracks and peered at Nius with a curious expression.

"You don't meet a lot of people here who know their Bible like that," Terry remarked.

Nius nodded back towards Adrian. "Be it known unto you therefore, men and brethren, that through this man is preached unto you the forgiveness of sins."

A split second passed before Terry's booming laughter rang out. The muscular priest bounded up the remaining steps while carrying Adrian as gently as an infant.

"Come on, guys." Nius waved the kids towards the

open doors as he swung his backpack onto a shoulder and ushered them into the church.

They went through to a large back area of the building which was filled with a random assortment of cots. The beds occupied much of the space and a few were already taken despite the early hour. Warm wood paneling covered the old walls. It was nothing special, but at the very least, not as dilapidated as the exterior.

Laying Adrian down onto a cot, Terry walked over to a large metal trunk settled in the corner and heaved the massive chest up and over to Adrian's bed. Graham and Steph sat near their father with sad but dry eyes. The priest worked methodically, removing Adrian's shirt and inspecting the various wounds. He cleaned and bandaged cuts as he went, stopping near a deep gash.

"This one needs stitches," Terry muttered under his breath to Nius before forcing his focused frown into a small smile for the kids.

"Graham, why don't you take Stephanie to the children's room. You two can play down there a while."

The boy opened his mouth to protest but looked at his sister and decided not to. The boy took her hand and led her towards a colorfully outlined door. Father Terry had already begun cleaning and sterilizing the wound for stitches.

*

Terry packed away his tools and first aid supplies and left Adrian to rest before beckoning Nius into his office. "Shut the door please."

Nius complied before setting his bag down, mind abuzz with questions. "What happened to this place?" was the first question to escape his lips.

"Our neighborhood?"

Nius shook his head. "Fenny. Every neighborhood, the whole city. I saw block after block of homeless laid out in streets surrounded by shuttered buildings."

Terry paused and looked at Nius curiously.

"Are you from around here?" Terry asked. "You lack the desperation that clings to the majority of people here."

"Not me. But I grew up listening to stories about this place from someone close. About how beautiful and safe the whole city was from the border to the ocean, with neighborhoods full of bustling happy people filled with pride."

"Whoever told you those stories must be talking about at least fifteen years ago." Terry spoke with sadness. "But the last five years have really felt like hell on earth."

"But why are even cops attacking innocent people—"

The huge man stood up like a shot. His chair toppled against the wall behind him and the desk lifted then slammed back onto the floor. The priest moved with such speed it surprised Nius, who flipped back and over the chair to stand at the ready.

"It was officers that attacked Adrian? You're positive? FPD?" Terry demanded with eyes bulging.

Nius stood, unsure, staring at Terry as he nodded yes.

"GO!" The giant man roared as he pointed to his door. The bellow was not angry but terrified.

What is happening? Nius wondered, shaken.

Terry looked strained and afraid. The priest's breathing was heavy as he struggled with what to do.

"If it was FPD, then they are already on their way and you can't be here," Terry nearly whispered and Nius strained to catch the man's breathless words. "I can't protect you when there are so many helpless here . . . I'm sorry." Terry wore his shame and sadness openly.

Nius was about to grab his bag when a huge bang rang out from the main hall. Terrified screams drowned out by bellowed orders to freeze filled the building. Terry seemed to shrink into himself. The huge man looked small and helpless.

"If I run out there, show them my face and take off running, will they leave everyone else alone?" Nius asked.

"Rationality flees from them when they feel attacked. I could never see some of my people again." Terry stood up as he spoke and adjusted his collar. Stepping around the desk he prepared to face the FPD.

"Ok then . . ." Nius replied hesitantly. The realization of what needed to be done nearly caused his head to spin. "I hope this isn't really stupid," he whispered before charging the door and kicking it wide open. He bolted towards the very surprised and very armed men.

Fewer than five officers had trickled into the empty sleeping area with the majority still securing the large worship hall where Terry held services. With fists clenched and stomach knotted, Nius charged the first officer. The man swung his baton but missed as Nius rolled forward under the strike and planted his hands against the floor. Pushing with his arms, he launched himself feet first at the men behind the first baton swinger. Striking the second officer in the midsection with both feet, Nius heard the man's gasp for air as the impact knocked the wind from his lungs and threw him backwards into the rest of the squad. Nius landed on his feet near the pile of officers and slid a baton free in an instant, hurling it at the first cop he had ducked. A sharp thud and grunt and the man crumpled to the floor.

Nius scanned the room searching for a window away from innocent people.

He sprinted toward the closest window as gunfire erupted all around him. Nius felt sick with sudden fear as he felt the tiny impacts of the assault rifle rounds grazing his skin for the first time in his life. Whatever barrier normally protected him had flinched slightly from the intense barrage of rounds. It was unlike anything he had ever experienced.

Bullets shredded the wood floor and paneling around him into tiny slivers, but he was just happy the police were firing in his general direction and away from the other parts of the church. Nius crashed through the glass followed by tracers and rounds. Falling towards the pavement, he slowed right before a painful impact and righted himself onto his feet.

"Put your hands behind your head or we open fire!"

Nius found himself surrounded by a sizable group of squad cars.

"This definitely turned out to be stupid," he conceded.

Nius eyed their guns and felt the unfamiliar sensation of true fear. He in no way wanted to test himself against the dozens of high-powered rifles aimed at him. Panic clouded his thinking while doubts surfaced and circled. He ached for Cheryl and the comfort of the woods, and nearly collapsed right there in his first taste of vulnerability.

The lead officer shouted, “Freeze! Do not move or I swear to God we will fire.”

Nius closed his eyes and took a deep breath while drawing comfort from somewhere unplaceable.

Raising an arm, the lead officer halted their movement and signaled guns at the ready instead.

For a few of the officers Nius must have seemed to vanish. He was simply gone in the fraction of a second it took for them to blink at the wrong moment. For those whose eye contact had remained unbroken, the truth was even harder to swallow. Dropping into a crouch, Nius jumped with incredible force. The leap fired him into the air like a slingshot as his stomach did uneasy flips. Though used to the forces from his jumps and antics, something about his abilities had changed and grown stronger.

What the heck?

Nius had intended to jump up and grab the church’s ledge but missed the building’s rooftop by several awkward feet and was left exposed for a few moments. The surprised officers who had followed his jump took the opportunity to fire at him. Whatever doubts Nius had felt about himself moments earlier disappeared. His supernatural protection deflected the barrage of bullets almost as if trying to prove itself once more.

Expecting his abilities to provide the usual soft

graceful landing as he came back down onto the roof, Nius was instead taken by surprise as he crashed headlong onto the rooftop in a twisted heap. Though unhurt, it was enough to disorient and surprise him as he crawled back onto his feet.

What is going on with me? Why couldn't I land like normal? Am I overtaxing myself? Can that happen?

Squad car sirens screamed as officers bellowed orders and organized in the streets below. With nightfall now obscuring the unfamiliar city, Nius realized any direction away from the church was a good direction. He spotted a neighboring building that stood much taller than the church. Nius eyed the distance and height. Lessons learned in the woods reminded him that altitude meant safety. First starting at the opposite end of the church roof, Nius dashed towards the larger building before trying to leap the monstrous expanse.

Nius felt his fear shift from worry he would not make the leap, to horror that he had overshot the entire building as he watched its rooftop sail past underneath him. Missing his intended target, he flew wildly towards the glass and concrete walls of the next building over.

This is going to suck. Nius gritted his teeth and braced for impact.

End over end, Nius smashed through a large glass pane and hit the floor awkwardly. His momentum carried him crashing through desks and partition walls as he rolled and bounced to a stop. Confused again by the lack of a slowed landing, Nius clambered to his feet and kept moving. Sprinting through the empty and eerily quiet building, he searched for a way out on the opposite side. He found another wall of windows and ran at the glass panes.

Tumbling through the air with shards of glass all around him, Nius could only hope he had enough momentum to get him to the next building.

Nius smashed through the next high-rise pane before hitting the floor harder than he had anticipated. He lay there among the glass shards, breath knocked out of him, attempting to gasp and suck in air. The far-off wails of police sirens sounded in the background. Nius had no choice but to give himself a few moments to catch his breath and assess his situation.

I'm three buildings over and at least twenty floors up, but where to now? I wish I hadn't come.

As the sirens in search of him grew more distant, Nius felt his body relax. The dark and quiet of the building covered him like a blanket. But something from his consciousness tugged at him and kept him from sinking beneath the dark waves of sleep.

Fwumph fwumph fwumph fwumph fwumph . . .

What's that noise?

It was more than a sound on the wind. He felt the reverberations deep in his chest and they shook away the restful quiet.

Fwumph fwumph fwumph fwumph fwumph . . .

Nius climbed to his feet. The strange thumping sound was now accompanied by a screaming engine that roared in his ears. Nius crept toward the shattered window to peer out and was suddenly blinded by brilliant floodlights. A sleek black helicopter with enormous mounted guns rose and hovered in front of the broken window.

Nius felt his heart pound in his chest as he squinted through his fingers. The powerful lights flooded the room and robbed him of his hiding place. Paper and debris flew violently around the vacant office as the helicopter's blades sliced heavily through the air.

Run!

Nius was unsure of whether he had heard the command or simply felt it.

As loud as the helicopter was, even louder was the terrifying sensation of fear that was not his emanating from within. Before he could ponder the faraway emotion that flooded him, another warning screamed in his mind.

Run!

Nius bolted desperately to his left. His first panicked

step propelled him onward as the spot where he had just stood exploded in a hurricane of deafening gunfire and shrapnel. The large high-powered rounds tore easily through the walls as if they were made of crackers.

If one of those hits me, it's over. I am dead. The realization that there were limits to his abilities was alarming.

Reaching the end of the hall and turning the corner, Nius was unsure of what he was looking for. He took another left and sprinted towards the center of the building hoping to gain some protection from the weapons behind the office building's internal walls. The strange inner voice urged him to an immediate stop, and he watched as a burst of bullets shredded the hallway he had almost run down. The thin partitions of the cubicles provided little cover for whatever gun they were firing.

Nius froze with his back pressed against the wall and panic rising. The light and shadows in the building shifted eerily as the police helicopter circled and the brilliant lights searched for him window to window. Pinpointing the helicopter's location by noise, he ran from its sound. He did not care where he ended up as long as it was out of range of that weapon. With adrenaline pumping and teeth clenched, Nius burst through an external window and out into the night once more.

Freezing air slapped and stunned him as his

protective force faltered. The chill wind now pierced through his clothes and numbed his skin as he fell toward the city streets below. Tears blurred his vision as the air rushed past. The cold he had never been forced to feel before dug into his bones now and blasted the breath from him. He spun and tumbled out of control as the ground rushed up to meet him.

I might die.

Images of Cheryl and Mona flared to life in his mind as dozens of memories filled with love and comfort flashed past. He relaxed his body and gave in to inevitability.

No.

It sounded so far away.

It felt so far away.

The scenes in his mind dimmed.

NO.

The word rang out powerful and clear. It sounded close enough have been spoken in his ear but Nius was still unsure he had heard it at all.

"No," Nius repeated.

Soft blue light danced behind his eyes and emanated a strength that his body seemed to hungrily absorb. Warmth reached his skin again and his vision cleared. The cold, whipping wind now flowed around him once more without touching him.

Only a few feet above the weathered asphalt, Nius felt his skin tingle and saw that it had the faintest glow. His fall slowed and his toes lightly touched down on the road.

The light vanished. The surge of strength and comfort was gone so abruptly, a hint of doubt flickered in his mind as to whether it had happened at all. He ducked into a nearby alley as the police helicopter continued circling the building he had just fallen out of. Nius huddled in the dark away from the main road behind piled garbage as one of the squad cars inched passed the mouth of the alley.

I need a place to stay I guess, he concluded after a few minutes of thought. He reached for his backpack straps and realized in horror that the bag containing all the money Cheryl had given him remained with Terry at the church.

Dammit.

A breeze picked up, bringing with it a sharp briny smell that swept away the stench of the garbage piled beside him. Nius closed his eyes and sucked in deeply through his nose. He climbed to his feet, knowing where to go. Jumping high and grabbing the ledge of the nearby single-story building, he eased himself onto the roof. He spotted what he was looking for in the distance.

Despite the situation, Nius felt a wave of joy at the sight of the distant ocean. Waves rolled on and on into the horizon. The waters near the shore reflected the beautiful lights of the city like twinkling stars you could almost touch. Without wasting a second, he leapt and easily cleared the distance to the next rooftop. He landed softly on his feet as his protection slowed his fall.

At least that's working now, he thought as he kept moving towards the ocean.

Running and jumping from rooftop to rooftop towards the sparkling expanse, Nius was gaining a feel for moving about this concrete and steel jungle. His steps came surer as he flipped and spun off of light posts and old billboards.

Almost feels like home. Nius grabbed the horizontal bar of a stoplight and swung himself up toward the roof of a nearby building. Sudden screeching tires caught his attention as a squad car below spotted him and pursued.

Picking up the pace, Nius ran across rooftops and away from the wailing police vehicle. The distant ocean waves drew closer as he ran through the darkness. He was confident he had lost the lone squad car that had spotted him. Sucking in another breath of the briny sea air, he exhaled it into the chill night. Distant sirens in the direction he had come from were the only sound on the wind as he moved.

Thwumpthwumpthwumpthwumpthwumpthwump thwump . . .

Nius froze at the sound as his body tensed with adrenaline. Looking behind him, he saw two separate searching lights in the distance racing towards him.

"Two now?" He groaned. He had barely survived against one, let alone two.

There was no burst of confidence or faraway voice this time to lend him will and strength. He ran for his life.

Reaching the beach, Nius finally leapt from the rooftops altogether and landed in soft sand illuminated by the brilliant white moon. Each running step on the shifting beach brought him closer to the waters.

Nius dove into the surf and pushed hard through the water as the sand behind him thudded with high-power machine gun rounds. The sound of heavy beating helicopter rotors pierced by thousands of tiny explosions from machine guns became muffled as he sank deeper beneath the waves.

Spinning around in the water, Nius looked back up towards the surface. He was barely able to make out the two brilliant floodlights now, as the helicopters circled and waited for him to resurface for breath.

With lungs aching for air, Nius exhaled his last breath and watched the escaping stream of bubbles rise before sucking in ocean water.

His lungs filled only with oxygen. The breath somehow remained water-free as it had in the lake. Nius kicked deeper down into the harbor depths and away from the searching lights, leaving a steady stream of bubbles in his wake.

CHAPTER 9

January 3rd
Monday Evening

Onur's post-whiskey head throbbed as he licked his dry mouth with a parched tongue. What little afternoon light there was that flitted into the apartment forced his eyes to squeeze shut. He rolled onto his stomach in an attempt to remove light from the equation before registering the noise that had woken him. On the mantle, his alarm filled the messy apartment with its loud beeps.

"Shuuuddup," he yelled into his pillow, the fabric and stuffing muffling his words.

The beeping continued and even rose in volume as if mocking him. He grabbed a hoodie off of the floor next to the couch and pulled it over his head in an attempt to continue sleeping. He groaned into the pillow again, his hangover and schedule for the day at complete odds with one another. The beeping soaked into the fabric wrapped around his head.

Why did I reprogram that damn clock?

After the conventional alarm clock had failed to rouse him one morning, Onur had gone to work on modifications for it—namely making sure it was loud, irritating, and would not stop unless he was completely awake.

With the hoodie failing to block out the noise, he slid himself into a semi-sitting position on the worn couch. His feet knocked over the empty beer cans that littered the floor.

Onur laid his head back as the usual stream of thoughts, schematics, and equations ran through his aching head, uncaring that the head they ran through would have preferred they not.

Raising both arms, he made fists that left both his middle fingers raised in the direction of the alarm clock that sat behind him. Small cameras Onur had installed read the gestures and silenced the incessant beeping.

Onur forced himself up off the couch and was immediately hit by a wave of nausea as his stomach rebelled against the copious amounts of alcohol imbibed the night before. Head throbbing, he took a deep breath and held it for a second to settle the churning. After a moment, he was able to shamble over to the end table and pick up the small device resting there. He brought it to his lips and sucked in deeply, filling his lungs with warm aromatic vapor.

His headache receded and his body relaxed as pleasant feelings filled his head. Even the light in the apartment stung less.

“Bit better,” he muttered.

Onur shuffled into the dimly lit adjacent room where a bank of dark monitors occupied one wall. They flared to life as he entered with a yawn.

His personally coded software monitored the city at its various levels, keeping an eye while he slept. It secretly connected to the majority of Fenny’s network, tracking everything from the subways to the high rises and everything in between. The screens were all connected to Onur’s docked laptop. It was a juggernaut of processing power of his own design and always ready to be grabbed and shoved into his backpack if the need to move arose.

“Play music, surprise me,” he spoke into the room. A thick rock drumbeat began to play. Though he had awoken dehydrated and needing the toilet at the same time, the computer room called to him first. Onur did not bother to resist the siren song of connectivity.

He slid into his chair and scanned the monitors,

checking his email and contacts before looking through Fenny's headlines for the day. Onur's hangover was pushed to the back of his head as he read words he never thought he would see.

"Religious leader Gene Nikko found dead: Suspected homicide." Onur whispered the words aloud to himself.

That was Herod's right-hand man. Top tier. Who on earth was able to get to him?

Suspicions had already begun to replace the happiness the news had brought. He flipped through his mental rolodex of folks in the city who would be happy to see Gene disappear but came up with no one who would be powerful enough to make a move on him.

Unable to pause his obsessive mind and celebrate this good news, he went to work. Onur launched several separate search windows before running off into the bathroom and relieving himself.

He ambled into his small kitchen and poured himself a large glass of orange juice. Being cheap in nearly every other respect was simply the result of being cash poor, but juice was a luxury he refused to skimp on.

"Was it Herod?" he wondered aloud. Maybe the priest had angered his own boss, but even that made little sense. Onur's knowledge of the secretive figure painted a much starker picture of what usually happened to Herod's enemies.

Gulping the sweet, pulpy juice, Onur returned to his monitors and scoured the results from the Fenicia Police Department network. He scrolled through recently submitted reports, finally finding what he was looking for. A double-click and it opened on the screen before him. Father Gene's full homicide file.

Herod never kills people with any worth to him. He just locks them up in that damn prison for the rest of their lives, Onur reasoned as he read and absorbed the details of the police report.

The only thing that kept Onur from just giving up and moving to another city was the knowledge that Herod would undoubtedly keep Jim alive on that island prison. His captive collection was no testament to his empathy or grace, but simply proof of his manipulative nature.

Viciously brilliant, Herod operated out of sight in the recesses of the machinery that was Fenny. Yet despite the man's invisibility, every gear and cog of Fenicia was greased with his money and influence. While most citizens would be unable to place a face to his name, if you had money or power, Herod already knew about you.

In the few short years he had been operating in the city, he had essentially become the city, and was now behind nearly every facet of Fenny's government. Of course, the last to fall had been the first to realize the danger: Jim Mallon and the FPD. Onur considered himself lucky not to be Jim's cellmate.

"Currently no suspects," Onur read, not knowing what to make of Gene's gruesome police report.

Though the prison operated on a closed network, Onur had discovered that criminals and those wanted by Herod were still booked through the police department computers before being taken to the island. This left a digital paper trail he could easily follow—at least until the transport boat landed on the island. After that point, everything was a complete information blackout.

"No suspects, no one in custody, no one wanted for questioning," he said aloud, his racing mind hitting a wall. "What in the hell killed him, a ghost?"

Digging deeper through the details of Gene's murder, Onur paused as a small window popped up on the screen, informing him an urgent alert had been issued to every officer out on the street.

"That's gotta be Gene's killer they are after."

Whoever had killed Father Gene was either working against Herod, working for Herod, or had no idea what they had gotten themselves into. While normally pragmatic, Onur allowed himself a tiny glimmer of hope that the man the FPD was after was capable. And more importantly, harbored just as much hate for Herod as Onur did.

Just the thought of trying to find and free Jim's captive family by himself made Onur want to crawl into a bottle again. Though it was unlikely, he found himself desperately grabbing at the possibility that he had found a partner. "The enemy of my enemy . . ." Onur whispered.

He checked the APB searching for a name but instead found it to be an address officers were being directed to. "22nd Epith, apartment 7."

That sounds oddly familiar.

And then his brain woke fully and the realization hit him.

"Holy shit, that's me!" he cried hoarsely as his eyes snapped wide in panic and his heart thumped like a jackhammer trying to escape his chest. He put both hands on the desk, pushed his chair back and rose to his feet. Anxiety flushed through him and threatened to become panic as he tried to collect himself.

"Seriously? I just got back from the warehouse a few hours ago and they already tracked me?"

He jerked the plugs out of the laptop and tossed it into his backpack. Onur pulled out his phone and flipped through the apps before hitting the small icon for Alton. Immediately, he connected to his robotic creation.

I just had to send him on surveillance duty, didn't I? Onur berated himself.

Miles away from the apartment, Alton rested on the rooftop of a building across from one of Gene's brothels watching and recording the people that came and went. As Onur studied the camera feed, he jabbed the number one button on the surface of his phone. The small robot recognized the touch tone and flitted off into the air towards his master.

Onur went in search of his shoes and heard a loud bang rattle the apartment door.

"Police! Let us in or we will use force to enter," they shouted through the door.

Though he'd fallen asleep the night before in jeans and a t-shirt, Onur stopped at his closet. He pulled on two more shirts over the one he currently wore. He jammed a rolled-up baseball cap into his pocket and slipped on a hoodie jacket before strapping on his backpack. He slid open the window to the old fire escape attached to the building.

Shoving his feet into his sneakers, he called out, "One minute. Be there in a second!"

He swung his leg over the windowsill and out onto the fire escape but suddenly stopped before pulling it back into the apartment.

He was forgetting something.

"My weed!" he cried under his breath. Onur ran to the cabinet holding up the old television and pulled out a sandwich bag full of pungent green marijuana buds.

Onur jerked in surprise as a tremendous impact rocked his apartment door. The officers were wasting no time in using their heavy iron door ram. Splintering open with a heavy crash, the door fell away revealing an abandoned apartment and an open window to the officers.

Grabbing his radio, one of the men reported in.

"Suspect fled out window. In pursuit and requesting backup. Suspect gray hoodie . . . backpack," Onur heard. He skipped the last few rungs of the fire-escape ladder and jumped down into the alley. Above him, two officers climbed out onto the fire escape. In the distance, the sound of sirens grew louder.

Onur pulled out his phone and tapped the icon to start the custom program he'd written. He went to work hacking the login portal for Fenicia's Public Works Department.

As the officers rushed down the first ladder, they slowed when they realized Onur wasn't running. "Look at this kid. Does he think we won't know it's him?"

The other officer snorted and they continued down the ladders, huffing and puffing with exertion. "Who cares as long as he makes it easy?"

Fingers a blur as he worked, Onur finally grinned. "Do either of you have a heart condition?" he yelled up to the officers earnestly. "I mean, nothing personal. I just worry."

One officer bristled and his hand rubbed the handle of his baton as both men stood on the platforms. "Boy, I'm going to hit you so hard in the mouth you're going to kiss your own ass."

"Okay . . . but I did ask." Onur waited until both officers' hands were touching the metal railing and then placed a small metal sphere on the bottom rung of the fire escape ladder.

One . . . two . . . Onur counted before a small beep sounded from the metal ball. Grunting in sudden pain, the two officers on the fire escape began jerking wildly before collapsing onto the steel platform.

Onur snatched the sphere off the ladder rung, slipped it into his pocket and ran out of the alley into the throng of people on the busy sidewalk.

*

Squad cars began swarming the streets and Onur slowed his pace on the bustling sidewalk to blend into the crowd like another shopper.

Navigating the public works system on his phone, he pinpointed what he needed and acted before looking towards the nearest intersection in time to see the fruits of his labor.

Without warning, the traffic lights began to change colors wildly. A line of police cars ran a red light that had been green just a second before, and Onur watched as one of the squad cars was t-boned by a sedan in the confused flow of traffic.

Quick-practiced motions had him slipping out of his hoodie and backpack. Onur stuffed the gray zip-up into his bag. Now wearing a black t-shirt, he slung the bag over a shoulder and continued walking with rest of the city, appearing as nonchalant as if he'd been strolling in the park on his way to feed some ducks. In reality, he felt panicky inside. He was waiting desperately for Alton to return so he could turn his phone to airplane mode, but he was at least happy to be putting distance between himself and his old apartment. Finally, a familiar buzz zipped by his head. A slight tug on the backpack let him know the small bot had settled inside an open pocket. He switched his phone's connections off.

So, what now? I'm homeless and I can't use my phone, just like old times.

It had been a long time since he had been this bad off. Without a secure apartment and safely connected computer or phone, it would be nearly impossible to hunt down the man needed for his tech modifications. And without new phone mods, he didn't dare connect to the cell network that Herod must have used to track him. It was a vicious circle.

I'm fucked. Stuck between a rock and a Mack truck.

With the morning's events still not making any sense to him, Onur couldn't stop his thoughts. How had Herod been able to track him? He always calculated carefully so that his methods left no trail, he'd made sure of that. Was it simply a coincidence that the night before, Onur had crashed Herod's warehouse?

It was a possibility, but the timing seemed too perfect, leaving him almost positive it was his involvement at the warehouse.

I really need to talk to Rodne. Which means I need my backup beta chip.

"Alton. Find Rodne and connect me. I'll be back online soon."

Alton launched skyward.

"Check the port!" he called after the AI.

The small robot changed direction and flitted towards the ocean at Onur's command. He watched as Alton left, the silver speck disappearing in the distance and leaving a small sadness in his heart before Onur shook his head.

Wow, that was pathetic. He mocked the sentimental feeling he had for the electronic creation.

Spotting Riba Bank close in the distance, Onur

quickened his pace. He wanted to secure a room before nightfall.

Owned by the wealthy Riba family for the last ninety-eight years, Riba Bank was one of the oldest institutions in Fenny. When the old patriarch and president Samuel Riba passed away, his children quickly changed the bank's course. Once a proud and honest family-owned bank run with principle, it seemed the newer generation of Ribas had a far different priority.

Money and only money.

Gone were the loans and mortgages for the working-class families to get ahead. Gone were the fairly priced student loans so that those in the city who wanted an education could work for one.

Though he hated that they specialized in money laundering for Herod, there was one service they offered that kept him a customer. Their self-service safety deposit boxes were renowned for lawlessness. While most banks required identification and supervision to open a safety deposit box, Riba bank made it clear they would not pay staff to hold your hand. Once rented, you were given the key with safety deposit box number etched into it. Customers could come and go as they pleased, without any troublesome witnesses or bank employees needing to be involved. If you had your key, you would be led to the safe room and left alone. No key, no access.

He approached the beautiful clear doors of the bank and his stomach knotted. A sizable group of armed security chatted on the other side of the glass like a bizarre gun-toting aquarium.

No one can possibly know who you are, he told himself, but sweat was beginning to bead on his forehead.

Paranoia convinced him the guards were staring him down suspiciously. Onur's eyes flicked up towards the group of security, his body tensing as he removed the keys from his pockets. Though the guards continued laughing and chatting, he couldn't shake the image of his bullet-riddled body bleeding out on the beautiful marble floors.

Onur approached the single teller behind the thick glass of the counter.

"Can I help you?" she asked.

"Yes, I was hoping to check my safety deposit box?" Onur held up his key as proof of belonging.

"Follow me." She led him towards the rear of the bank, and they entered a hallway with rows of doors. Onur jumped slightly as they walked past the first room, its door swinging open abruptly as a heavy-set tattooed man burst out. The bearded man eyed Onur but relaxed when he saw the bank employee with him.

Onur couldn't help but notice his comically bulging pockets.

Entering one of many vaults in the building, Onur slid his key into the safety deposit box, enjoying the heavy satisfying click as the mechanism responded. He slid the box out of the wall of the vault, turning back towards the employee.

"Did you want a viewing room or are you good just taking your stuff?"

"Viewing room please."

At the end of the hallway, she waited for Onur to enter one of the secure rooms before shutting the door behind him.

He looked around the room in distaste. Weak fluorescent light seemed to die against the gray walls making the room dark. Onur set his box on the table and snapped open the clasps while keeping the lid closed.

Regardless of the bank's claims that viewing rooms were private, Onur knew better. Sensors built into his phone had previously warned him of at least a camera and microphone hidden in the paneling.

Onur sank into a soft office chair and pulled the box towards him before reaching inside blindly. His fingertips felt slips of paper before brushing against a small metal and plastic piece in the corner of the box. He shoved the concealed microchip and fistful of money into his pocket, leaving the empty box behind.

At just under $3,000, the cash in the safety deposit box represented his entire savings.

Back outside, Onur plopped down onto a park bench with a street cart hotdog. The sky was burning a dusky orange. He'd woken later than he realized. Onur wiped his fingers free of mustard before pulling out his phone and removing the small chip inside. He cracked the SIM card into tiny pieces before letting them fall down a grate.

Back to anonymous. Onur snapped the chip from the safety deposit box into the phone.

Using the city's network without his special SIM cards would have been impossible, let alone hacking government services.

He searched out Alton's signal on his rebooted phone, pinpointing it to the docks before connecting to his robotic creation. "Find him?"

<Yes>

Alton's response flared across his screen.

"You rock. Connect me."

"Hey, Onoor!" Rodne greeted.

Onur groaned and shook his head as Rodne put way too much ethnic accent on his name.

If he weren't such an idiot, it would be racist.

"I would recognize this little guy anywhere. Change your mind about selling his schematics?" Rodne asked.

"You wouldn't even know where to begin building him. Listen, I'm looking for something you can help me with," Onur replied to head off any more banter.

"What you need, I got it! I got the dankest buds in just yester—"

Onur stopped him with an upheld hand.

"Still packing with the last sack you got me."

"I live to please."

"I'm actually in the market for an apartment."

"You had a nice place, hacked bank loan, no? Them was some sweety digs . . ." Rodne said, letting the sentence hang. Onur knew him well enough to understand that he was asking what happened without actually asking what happened.

"Yeah, they got to it."

"And you got away? Damn, you good."

"Probably just lucky," he sighed, not wanting to get into details with night falling fast.

"I know of a two-bed right across from a park."

That sounds way too nice . . . "Amazing, where at?"

There was a pause before Rodne answered. "Black and Yellow Park."

"Are you joking?" Onur was not sure how to feel. Fifteen years ago, Hampshire Court was a beautiful and expensive area to live in, but now it consisted of slums and projects converted from the old apartments.

Working poor families just trying to survive while being forced into the same dilapidated buildings as addicts, gangbangers, and murderers. The unending placement of black and yellow crime tape everywhere gave rise to the morbid nickname. On the one hand, it was definitely an area that Herod had written off as garbage. Most of the crime committed was either for food or drug money. Dying because of whatever was in his pockets, though, would be just as awful as being caught by Herod.

Onur knew his choices were limited. “Internet?”

“Yes.”

“I’ll take it.”

“Great! I’ll set it up. That’s $900 up front. Just meet me at 146 Galile Street in an hour.”

“And Rodne? I want my tools back.”

“Oh ho ho, coming out of retirement?”

“Something like that.” He stood and waved down a junker taxi.

*

Onur stepped out of the yellow cab and took in his new neighborhood. Garbage and empty bottles dominated the dirty streets while huge potholes dotted the road like meteor impacts. In the alley across the street was a group of scowling gangbangers drinking out of brown paper bags.

Neighbors seem nice.

You must have looked gorgeous ages ago, he thought as he stared at his new building. Though dirty and rundown, it was beautiful art-deco architecture. The old paint job was faded but reminiscent of its former glory. Looking up at the top floor, Onur nearly lost his nerve with the move. A portion of the apartment building's roof had collapsed and was covered by a thin blue tarp.

"Onooor! Like your new place?" Rodne asked, coming from around the corner of the building.

"It's pronounced Onur, like in 'honor thy mother.' You don't have to put so much accent on it."

Rodne ignored the often-repeated request and changed the subject ensuring that nothing would differ next time. "Checked about the internet."

"You said it already had internet."

"Well, I was pretty sure at the time—"

Onur's look stopped him mid-sentence.

"But you're sure now, at least?"

"Oh, yeah. Technically, the building has internet. But . . . the power to the whole building is currently out."

Onur took a deep frustrated breath.

"Temporarily! Carl the owner is on it. Just waiting on some back rents to fix it."

Onur rolled his eyes. This apartment at least offered

him shelter in a city that was lacking. He could make do while he planned. Finding whoever killed Father Gene was top priority, which made this living situation the best for staying out of Herod's hands.

"You got the $900?"

"No electricity? I'll give you seven."

Rodne frowned but gave a curt nod. "Fine."

Handing over the wad of cash, Onur held his hand out expectantly. Rodne dropped the heavy gym bag on the ground and handed him a key.

"I'm shocked. I asked you to hold onto my tools and you actually still have them. Couldn't find any buyers?"

Rodne looked pleased with himself.

"Didn't look for any, I figured you would ask for them back. Would have been like selling Michelangelo's chisel."

Rodne eyed the gangbangers across the street.

"There's the key. Apartment 22. Call me when you need more bud." Rodne rushed across the street towards the gang members. "Fellas! Got new shit in, you guys interested?"

Judging by the jubilant responses, Onur guessed they were repeat customers.

Onur entered the building's dark hallway and walked toward the elevator, but nearly tripped on an old ratty sneaker. From what little conversation he could pick out, these apartments seemed to be mostly occupied by families, which made the lack of electricity even more depressing.

Richest country on Earth and they live like third world.

He spotted the breaker box near the elevator but hoped he would not need it. Onur held his breath as he stood in front of the elevator doors and pressed the up button.

It did nothing.

Not even backup power for the elevator. Great.

"We haven't had power for a week. Even when they fix it, just goes out again after a few days," said a pleasant voice behind him.

A young black girl stood in the doorway of the nearest apartment rocking a toddler.

"Yeah, it didn't look very promising."

"At least they leave the gas on. You can still heat and cook," she said with a shrug.

She stepped further into the hallway and Onur was hit with a wave of delicious smells and warm spices. Hunger gnawed at him but he pushed food from his mind by focusing on work.

"You moving in?" she asked.

"Yup."

He had already begun to calculate voltages while piecing together the electrical layout of the building.

"Then I'm sorry for your luck."

It took Onur a few distracted seconds to realize the sarcastic joke and laugh.

"Well, I have to put this little guy to sleep. It was nice meeting you. My name's Candice."

"Onur," he replied, giving her a wave goodbye as she slipped back into her apartment.

Nice neighbors, he thought once again but without a trace of sarcasm this time.

Onur unzipped the gym bag revealing a large assortment of tools and smaller tool sets. He switched through the modes of his multimeter to make sure the batteries were still functional.

He then pulled out a small steel bar and pried the door to the breaker box open. The repair work was calming and relaxing to his tired mind. Having his tools back was soothing.

Thirty minutes later, Onur wiped his brow and dropped a screwdriver back into the bag. He stared down the now pitch-black hallway and flipped the main breaker as he held his breath.

The lights flickered before flaring to life. A few cheers came from behind some of the apartment doors, the tenants obviously happy with the restored power.

Onur turned and hit the up button on the elevator. He began to pack up his tool bag when he was overwhelmed with a familiar delicious smell. A beaming Candice stood in her doorway holding a Tupperware container.

"You fixed it! Thank you. That means a lot to everyone here."

The smell wafting from her apartment proved too much for him and his stomach loudly groaned in protest.

"Sorry."

"You have nothing to apologize for." She handed him the Tupperware filled with hot food.

Uncomfortable with being thanked he shrugged. "I needed the electricity too."

"I want that Tupperware back when you're done."

"If I don't eat it too," he joked.

Candice shook her head and laughed, shutting the door behind her.

Onur balanced the container delicately as if it held precious gems. He gathered his belongings and stepped into the lift.

In a moment, the doors parted again with a blast of chill wind.

"Of *course* this is my floor."

The long hallway ended abruptly in jagged edges of burnt wood and the flapping blue tarp that failed to keep out the elements. He scanned door numbers, praying his apartment was on this end of the hallway. At least he got his wish in that.

Onur entered and tried to lock the door behind him. "That's going to need some work."

Broken chain locks hung from the wall beside the frame. Their opposite ends had been ripped from the previous front door and hung uselessly, the building owner apparently too lazy or too cheap to repair.

Onur placed the Tupperware down on the carpeted floor and dug through his bag before pulling out two thick chain locks still in their original packaging from the hardware store.

After having jumped from apartment to apartment his entire life, Onur's hands moved with practiced motions as he screwed the locks into the door. Satisfied with his temporary repair, he decided it was safe enough to eat.

His eyes flicked about the room, first, as he searched for an accompanying power outlet. After spotting one nearby, he wrestled between desires.

Even hunger lost out to his compulsion for connectivity.

He lugged both bags into the room and plugged his laptop in. He flipped through his cellphone and booted one of his many homebrew-protected wifi apps before accessing the building's network and connecting his laptop to it.

Though able to easily access the city's infrastructure on his phone, it lacked the processing power and memory needed to force his way into the more secure systems. Plus an actual keyboard just *felt* better. Onur was immensely curious about what the FPD had been up to since his departure from his former address.

A few minutes of standard chatter revealed no new information and Onur's hunger finally began to gain the upper hand. He was about to grab the container when an emergency alert flashed across the FPD communications software.

"What the hell . . . ?"

ALL PERSONNEL TO REPORT TO 15th STREET AND ALTUM. SUSPECT FOR GENE NIKKO'S DEATH TO BE TAKEN ALIVE. SURVEILLANCE VIDEO SECURELY EMBEDDED FOR ID.

Onur dove for the keyboard and clicked the video link in the message, his eyes glued to the screen as the short clip played.

The girl on the screen was pretty, dressed in jeans and a plain shirt as she scooped money from a mangled ATM machine. The video was only a few seconds long and Onur played it again. His mind raced through hundreds of questions, most of them about the state of the hardened steel ATM that appeared to have been ripped apart by her.

"That's her then," he whispered, the image on the screen completely and utterly at odds with what he had expected. "Is this for real? Does this shit happen?" He recalled comic-book memories from the depths of his childhood.

With no time to waste, Onur snatched his phone off the floor and dug through his bag for a few of the small spheres. He ran towards the front door but paused as he reached for the handle. A small urge of self-preservation had forced its way into his mind.

You don't have to do this. Every single cop is already on the way and they want you bad . . .

His hesitation lasted only a second when he remembered his promise to Jim. "Alton!"

The small robot crawled from the backpack, flitted into the air and landed on Onur's hand. Its legs wound around Onur's wrist and the small robot shifted into a watch.

Onur couldn't help but look back at the container of food forlornly. "Soon, beautiful. I promise," he said to the stew.

CHAPTER 10

January 3rd
Monday Evening

Herod entered the garage elevator and pressed for his penthouse. The panel came alive requesting biometric clearance. Herod pressed his thumb against the small black pad under the screen and waited a few seconds while his identity was confirmed. A deep vibration traveled momentarily through the elevator as the cable locks released and the lift rose.

While the rest of the building was split into different arms of Herod's operation, the entire top floor was exclusively Herod's penthouse, complete with a personal garden and pool that dominated the building's rooftop. As the elevator dinged his arrival to the top floor, its doors slid open revealing a beautiful and spacious foyer of white marble accented by wrought silver.

His foot barely had crossed the threshold before a kind voice greeted his arrival. “Welcome home, sir.” Turning the corner in a crisp tailored outfit was one of Herod’s assistants. Though by all accounts they were butlers if not outright servants. “Norman deposited a man in the spare wine cellar and instructed two of your security to guard him. Norman is currently showering and I took the liberty of having his suit sent to be dry cleaned and pressed. His clothing will be waiting for him along with instructions to wait for you in the office.”

“Perfect, thank you, can you get Charlie on the line in the office?”

The servant’s lips pressed together at the mention of Charlie. His dislike for the eccentric genius engineer was as obvious on his face as everyone else’s. The help nodded curtly and walked away towards the main office.

It wasn’t surprising that nearly everyone who met Charlie loathed the man. Not one to waste precious brain synapses, Charlie truly cared nothing for others and did his best to let everyone know. That, combined with his paranoid schizophrenic delusions regarding alien conspiracies, had rendered him impossible to deal with, at least until Herod had installed “The Nanny.” Herod used the ankle- monitor medication injector to properly treat the man’s condition—and “properly” meant keeping him not so medicated that the chemicals dulled the man's senses, but enough that he didn't fall into a state of psychosis. There was no one on the planet who understood firearms and weapons like Charlie, and he did his best work while stumbling along the divide between medicated and a danger to himself. Thanks to his designs, the FPD carried some of the most advanced and powerful guns on the planet. But Herod wanted the envelope pushed. He wanted innovations that leapt ahead of current technologies. Herod wanted energy weapons.

Yet as obsessed and driven as Charlie was about guns, he had little interest in Herod's vision of the future of fighting. If it didn't use a powerful explosion or device to propel a nearly molten metal slug, then it was a waste of time to the engineer.

Letting himself sink into one of the soft leather couches, Herod rested his head back. A small, tired sigh escaped his lips while he waited.

I left him at the bottom of my priorities far too long. I have been busy. No, that's not exactly true. I just didn't want to deal with him.

His renewed interest in Charlie's work was no coincidence.

I have no idea what Ann can do and not the slightest clue what she is capable of. We might really need Charlie's specialty now.

Footsteps alerted Herod to an approach. He watched as the help entered the foyer with a face red and pinched in anger.

"I had to make several attempts, but I have him on his private channel. He is . . . agitated at the interruption."

Herod walked down the hall passing by the precious works of art that lined his walls. Reaching the burnished wooden door of his office, he stepped through and squinted. The bright evening sun streamed in through the immense windows overlooking the city.

Herod settled into his large black office chair and reached for the small electronic tablet resting on the desk. He flipped through a few options and slid his finger across the screen. Following his swipe, the motorized blinds behind him shut. With the obtrusive glare now gone, he entered his password. Charlie's unkempt and impatient face appeared on the screen.

"You shouldn't press my attendants' buttons like that, Charlie. You set them off for the entire day and then dinner is terrible."

"Then eat out or order in. But you send them after me and I can't be held responsible for what I say to them."

Herod smiled a mirthless smile and made Charlie fidget. "Come on, Charlie. I will always hold you responsible for your actions. You know that."

The irritation left Charlie's eyes as he nodded his

agreement. Herod knew better than to think this signaled Charlie's full cooperation, however, aware that at any moment the man was capable of erupting into a shower of curses and rage. What little obedience Herod managed to frighten and threaten into Charlie was short lived and counted in minutes. The man's demons, ego, and untreated psychotic episodes were uncontainable.

"I want updates, Charlie. I want to be kept informed. I want to know what my money and resources are being spent on. Don't make me repeat myself every time I speak to you."

Charlie was about to respond when Herod's eyes flicked up towards his office door. Norman stood in the doorway, showered and now wearing a clean suit.

"Come on in, Norm. I was just chatting with Charlie."

Norman's usually inscrutable face revealed deep distaste. Herod nearly laughed at the universal opinion of his weapons engineer. Nodding for the engineer to continue, Herod waved Norman behind him.

"Oh, look. It's Asshole Mountain. I thought you were the pervert's errand boy," Charlie remarked.

Not even one minute, Herod groused silently.

"Gene is dead," Herod interrupted before Norman could retort. "It's all over the news. You don't keep yourself very informed, do you?"

For once, Charlie was silenced. His eyes widened

as if he had been slapped and he mouthed words that didn't come before finally sputtering out a sentence.

"It's not that I am trying to avoid you, Herod. I swear to you I'm not. I get busy . . . and you just saw how behind on things I can be . . . Please, please . . ." Charlie's rising panic was obvious as sweat formed near his temples.

Herod almost wanted to keep him terrified but dismissed the thought.

"It wasn't me. Calm down."

Charlie now appeared curious rather than embarrassed. Herod wasn't convinced the man was capable of shame.

"What the hell happened? Some poor girl's father get fed up with him?"

"Don't worry about that. It doesn't concern you. I called about something else very important and we should both be hoping you have good news. Do you have a prototype?"

Charlie sat as still as he could, but Herod's keen eyes picked out the subconscious jaw clench. Charlie's right shoulder also bounced as his foot tapped nervously against the floor.

"There is still some research that needs to . . ."

"Don't." Herod spoke sharply. "You have spent millions of my money over the course of a year. I own the companies you order equipment and raw materials from. You have been defying direct orders and building whatever you please. I have given you leeway, Charlie, we have history—"

"Is that what you call it? History? My guns made you."

"And my money, industrial plants, and factories made your guns. So it would seem I made myself."

Charlie glared but said nothing.

"Your designs are brilliant, but I need you to understand that things are different now. Things are happening and we are in danger. You need to abandon your current projects."

"Don't you get it? That is what they want! Don't you think their ships will be built with shields for energy weapons? They will have thousands of years to be better at energy technology and weapons and . . ."

"Enough!" shouted Herod, silencing Charlie's frantic rant. "I am sick of listening to your paranoid delusions regarding some nonexistent future alien war. I allowed your eccentricities because in your madness you provided me the most advanced and powerful guns on the planet."

Charlie nodded.

"There is no more option in this Charlie. There is no wiggle room, no leeway, and most importantly no time.

I will provide whatever resource you need and you will build a functioning prototype in the next few weeks. If you refuse as you have there will be no games of phone tag, no millions to dedicate to your caveman weapon research."

"You'll kill me." Charlie finished for Herod.

"Oh no. I would never think of killing you, Charlie."

The brilliant engineer narrowed his eyes in suspicion at the unexpected response. Herod flashed his smile with eyes cold and disconnected from the grin he wore.

"I would have you hunted down like an animal. Chained up in the smallest room you have seen. You would sleep in your own filth and I would hide you from death. I would force sustenance into your body as your mind and soul beg me to let you leave this world."

Herod kept his tone earnest rather than threatening.

"I would keep you there until your last breath escaped your body. Picking your brain clean of every design and thought."

Charlie remained silent, his eyes shifting back up to Norman as the large man picked the perfect time to stretch to his full height. Herod broke the silence with a voice so charming and genial it was disarming.

"Or you finish the prototype and create plans for outfitting one of my plants for mass production and oversee the upgrades. After that, I don't care if you build a gun that fires guns. As long as you also continue improving on my energy weapon."

Charlie slumped in defeat.

"The basic research is done. I have found a suitable power source but there is an issue with size and weight."

"Begin building them. I will find the men to carry and fire them and if I can't find them, I will make them out of weaker ones."

Charlie nodded his compliance before disconnecting the call.

Herod sat back in his chair as he stared at the blank screen for a few seconds before finally nodding his approval after digesting every detail of the meeting.

"Thank you, Norman. You were the perfect emphasis."

The big man said nothing.

"Are you hungry?" Herod did not wait for a response, instead firing a quick text message requesting a small dinner be served for two. It was an odd understanding Herod had of people. He was always able to anticipate decisions and behaviors, but he seemed to lack some crucial understanding of Dave's *why*. Even now with Dave beaten, drugged, and starving, the man refused to tell Herod everything he knew about Ann. As far as Dave knew he would never again be free or even alive if he didn't cooperate. Yet he still refused to talk.

What misguided part of him continues protecting an orphan he has no real connection to?

"Dinner should be served any minute. Walk and talk with me. I have a lot of questions." Herod insisted.

"What would you like to know?"

"I have to admit, Norm, I miss that about you. No bitching or whining, just straight to business."

Norman remained silent as they made their way down the hall from Herod's office. Taking the left at the end of the hall into an opulent dining room, they settled into stylish chairs.

"All right then. When did Father Gene send you? I assume yesterday morning so that you could make your move during the announcement about Jim."

Norman nodded his agreement as he bit into a thick turkey sandwich and closed his eyes as he chewed.

"We caught up to them around Khave's coffee. That's about where Dave tried to have them make a break for it."

Herod straightened in his chair with curiosity.

"Did you see anything odd about the girl? Anything at all?"

"I didn't see what she did. I was further back while Nick ran them down into an alley. I heard his scream though . . . It was an awful shriek." Norman shook his head as if trying to loosen the memory of the sound. "By the time I got there, his hand was missing and he was gushing all over the place."

Norman put his sandwich down with a puzzled look on his face.

"She looked just as bad for the wear. Her head was bleeding and she was nearly unconscious when I used the drug on her."

"I can guarantee you that whatever she did left much deeper scars than Nick did," Herod muttered before continuing his questioning.

"And Dave. Anything different about him?" Herod asked.

Norman shrugged, the small movement summing up his opinion of Dave.

"What happened after?"

"I brought the car around and dragged all three into it before heading to Gene's. He took the girl, took Nick, and told me to get rid of Dave."

"How much drug?" Herod asked.

"On the girl? A whole syringe," Norman replied.

Herod's eyes widened in surprise.

"A whole syringe? Of Inydyne? That is something to consider."

"And she was starting to come to when we arrived. Gene needed another dose to keep her out."

Tapping his spoon's handle against the table, Herod

brooded over this information. "When she was waking, before Gene was able to dose her, did she say anything?"

Norman thought for a few seconds before shaking his head no.

Damn.

"There was something else though. Her eyes." Norman paused as he appeared to struggle with his memory. "They fluttered when she tried to wake and . . ." He pushed the dinner plate away. "I saw black."

"You mean you passed out?" Herod asked.

"No. In her eyes . . . I saw black. In her eyes. The white, everything, it was . . ."

"Were you shining any light on her face? Flashlight? Ceiling lights in the car?"

"No flashlight, I could see well enough. It was a long drive and my eyes adjusted. The eyes were black. Just . . . black." Norman finished.

Herod became quiet. Seconds stretched into a full minute.

"What I struggle with is why did Gene continue for her in the first place? I made it very clear what would happen if I found out. She simply beat me to it." Herod wondered.

Norman shook his head in disbelief.

"It was the girl that killed him? You know that absolutely?"

"I don't use absolutes. I believe it was the girl, however. There are currently no others." Herod noticed the man downing a beer from a bottle he had not heard open. Herod didn't buy twist-top.

Must have used his hand. Fucking bull moose.

Herod couldn't help but recall Gene sprawled out on his own rape room floor with throat ripped out. It was a small sense of comfort to have the powerful Norman close by for more than his brute physique. Herod knew and understood Norman. There were no surprises to him after so many years.

He is reliable and that is something I need right now.

"With Gene gone, I'm going to want your services again."

"Then I want my family released." Norman bartered.

Herod laughed outright.

"See. We already know each other so well!"

Norman was not laughing.

Before the first streams of dawn's light, Herod had learned of Gene's death and Norman's involvement. His people had been quick to find and bring Norman's family as bargaining chips.

"Your family is in the building and after this is taken care of, you can see them. I'm looking forward to having you in my employ again. Hopefully this time we can avoid the unpleasantness that forced me to have you work for Gene these last two years. There is no more Gene and that leaves you with very few options. Two, really."

Norman said nothing, instead reaching for another beer.

Herod left the dining room and headed to his office once again. The room was now dark in the waning light as the sun disappeared from the horizon. Once inside, he pressed the slick button on the wall panel engaging the door locks. He enjoyed listening to the heavy thuds and feeling the vibrations as multiple locks around the door engaged.

He redialed the missed call he had ignored during his dinner with Norman. "Yes?"

Herod jerked the phone away from his ear as he was assaulted by the wail of police sirens and wind.

"Herod?" came his police captain's drowned-out voice. "I was on my way when you didn't answer. We have a hit on her location. Security footage for an ATM. Sir, you . . . You have to see this. I'm sending the clip of security feed now and our intercept team is en route."

Herod ended the call without another word and stared at the screen. His excitement grew as the video began to play.

CHAPTER 11

January 3rd
Early Monday Morning

The sharp cold bit through her thin layers. Her shirt and jeans were too wet to provide much warmth. Between the numbing chill of the rain and lingering effects of whatever they had injected her with, Ann could barely feel her skin. Shivers rattled her body as it attempted to generate warmth. Stumbling over an uneven edge of concrete, she caught herself and cursed into the night. She was somewhere in Fenicia, but where? There were just blocks and blocks of empty rundown buildings devoid of light or landmarks. Streetlights and traffic stops were dead and covered in years of grime.

Lacking a destination or plan when she ran from the house, Ann moved quickly and slowed only when forced into the shadows by patrolling FPD squad cars. They would stop a young girl at this time in this neighborhood, and with her arm and clothes tainted by Gene's blood she couldn't imagine anyone worse to run into.

Her fear and distrust for Fenicia's police department had not always been there. However, four years of watching their irrational harassment of Dave escalate for reasons she never understood—and he would never tell her—had cemented it.

A low engine rumble echoed down the street and headed towards her, the tires crunching over gravel-filled potholes in the darkness. Ann ducked into an alley and hid behind piles of uncollected garbage as the FPD squad car slowly rolled by with lights off.

Having trudged for blocks in wet socks that slapped inside her sneakers, Ann found it difficult to rise to her tired feet again. The freezing dark alley felt practically inviting compared to the open streets. Ann knew it was a temporary safety but couldn't resist a moment's rest.

Just a few minutes and then I keep going, she promised.

Dave should have tried harder.

The thought came from nowhere and yet rang clear.

"That's . . . that's not right." Ann responded to no one as she sat up awkwardly. In all her years she had never felt that way about Dave.

Only silence answered her.

That's not true! she thought angrily, forgetting that the emotion triggered things she did not understand.

The unfamiliar thought had struck her as uncharacteristically selfish. Dave had always done everything in his power for her. He had even attempted to confront her kidnappers by himself to buy her enough time to escape. The sacrifice, devotion, and care he had shown Ann stood as her definition of love in this world.

Ann clambered up, her exhaustion squashed by her anger at the unwelcome notion that Dave had not done enough.

If after everything we have been through, I give up now . . . then the only person to be angry at is me. I should have tried harder.

Compared to the despair she had been feeling, the anger was almost a comfort. It masked her fear and her doubts as she clung to it, unwilling or unable to deal with the tidal wave of grief that would surely pull her under.

"I should have killed them." As soon as she spoke the words through gritted teeth, she regretted them and felt her hatred leave.

Though her own anger had dissipated, a strange disconnected heat-rage flooded her. The chill in her skin evaporated as her body warmed. Ann reached down and squeezed the hem of her shirt. Cold, dirty water leaked between her fingers from the soaked fabric but somehow did not touch her skin. Breathing a small sigh of relief, she wiggled her toes, recalling how just a few minutes ago they had been completely numb.

But the peculiar rage did not stop and continued to build until Ann felt herself shaking. The pleasant warmth turned uncomfortable and feverish as licks of steam rose from her clothes. She almost cried out as the temperature rose and the rain in her clothing hissed against her skin like a griddle.

As suddenly as it had washed over her, the emotion was gone, leaving Ann empty and confused in the darkness. Her much dryer clothes no longer steamed and her skin was no longer on fire. Ann looked herself over as her hands felt down her arms, seeing no burns or damage whatsoever.

Am I going crazy?

Knowing she had to move, Ann pushed questions from her mind as she looked out at the dim street for FPD. She peered back behind her into the alley and weighed her options. The alleyway was cloaked in a darkness she could not penetrate with her eyes, meaning no one looking for her would be able to either. Deciding to take her chances in the tight winding gaps between the buildings, Ann disappeared into the darkness.

It isn't acting the same anymore. Everything is changing.

For most of her life, Dave and Ann had treated her unusual abilities as if they were a hiccup or sneeze—temporary distractions and problems to be dealt with in the moment.

Peering ahead, Ann spied a light. The towering walls gave way to what looked like small back porches lined with the packed dirt of old yards. The lone light seemed out of place after her long trek through several abandoned blocks. Passing beneath it, Ann had a better view of the row of small decaying houses whose back porches lined the alleyway. The air hung heavy with cigarette smoke as well as a thicker, more potent smell that seemed to cling to everything.

Her steps came quicker now. This area had a lived-in feeling that was becoming more sinister with every passing second. Without warning, a sudden movement from all around her made it too late to turn and run the way she came.

Dressed in heavy hoodies and jackets with various boots and sneakers, they closed in and cut off her entrance and any exit that might have occurred to her. They wasted no time pretending personal space meant something.

"Hey, girl, what're you doin' around here?"

"Where you heading so fast?"

"Hold up there. Give us a minute. You look like a fine payday."

Their voices dripped with a sarcasm as if their horrible plans were an unspoken joke. A wave of revulsion washed through Ann for far too many times that night. She felt a rising fear, though something in her recognized that the fear was on behalf of the men.

Stay calm, breath, deep breath, she ran through mantras trying to keep a cool head.

They are going to bind you up again and take you back unless you kill them . . .

Ann's hands clenched into fists at the internal goad that sounded nothing like her.

"Ey, Chooch, grab the bitch before she books it. Gene's been wantin' more girls."

One of the smaller men who must have been "Chooch" approached her.

Calm, stay calm, deep breaths, Ann repeated. Slight electric tingles raced through her skin as the man walked behind her and placed his hands on her shoulders.

They don't deserve the breath they take . . . Stop their breathing . . .

Again, the frightening thought turned her stomach and inflamed that disconnected fury even as she tried to calm herself. Knowing that there weren't many outcomes, she realized that her only salvation rested in her little-understood abilities. She could recall the horror of blood-soaked walls and the priest's torn throat in her hand.

I killed him and I don't even remember it.

One of the others stepped in front of her, grinning.

"No reason to be shy, this should be quick."

"I agree," Ann said coldly. There was going to be a terrible scene that she was powerless to avoid.

"So here's what's gonna happen. We tie you up nice and pretty." He mimed tying a bow. "Then we make a call to Gene and make dollars off your ass."

They obviously didn't know Gene was dead, and it was best if it stayed that way.

Her fists clenched.

The heat-rage building inside Ann was now her own. Dave was gone. Her life with him was destroyed. Everything had been taken by the utter piece of garbage that was Gene.

Ann pointed a finger at the man who uttered Gene's name. "You know Gene?"

Ann marched towards him with purpose as he backpedaled. Chooch and the other men tried to hold her back but could not. Grabbing her arms, they pulled and heaved with all their strength only to find themselves dragged with each step as if they were a plastic bag around her ankle.

As Ann reached the man, he moved to choke her throat but she grabbed the hand and tugged him downwards so she could clutch his neck instead. Ann could feel her lips twist into a smile that was not hers. With inhuman strength, she pulled his arm down while also forcing his neck up. He screamed in agony as tissue reached the limits it could stretch.

Rip him in half . . .

Horrified, she instead released the man's wrist and neck and grabbed him by the front of his jacket and launched him at the other thugs, all of them collapsing in a heap. The rest of the men backed away uneasily as she paused to try and gather her jumbled and still-violent thoughts.

Scrambling to their feet again, they pulled out knives and guns and aimed them at her, and Ann felt as if her better instincts were about to lose control.

"Hey now, what's going on down there?" The thugs started in alarm as the deep voice echoed off of the houses.

"It's fucking Terry. Move it. We need to be gone," one of the gang members said. The others agreed.

Slipping into houses and smaller walkways that branched off, the gang members disappeared, leaving

Ann standing alone. She nearly fell over as the heat-rage left her and exhaustion set in.

A large man dressed in black slacks and a thick, unbuttoned coat approached her. His priest's collar was openly displayed. "Are you ok, miss? Did they hurt you?"

The sight of the collar made her mind flash to Gene. Her stomach dropped. She backed up several steps and Terry raised his hands and stopped.

"Easy now. I'm not here to frighten or upset you."

Ann continued staring at him silently but stopped backing away as he attempted to talk.

"They didn't hurt you? No cuts, no bruises, you're ok?"

Ann allowed him a nod letting him know she was all right.

Terry smiled wide with relief at hearing the good news. "Well good. If there aren't any immediate concerns, you should be heading home. It's much too early to be late."

Ann tensed at the mention of home.

He removed his own jacket and tossed it to her. Ann caught it easily. The soft fabric smelled of sweet bread better than anything she remembered in her favorite coffee shops. Bringing the coat close, she breathed the wonderful aroma in deeply and Terry laughed at the high praise.

"I find baking a really good homemade coffee cake is a great way to get people's butts in the pews of my church," he said.

"Why? Is your message a lie?"

Terry's laugh stopped short as he thought about her question. "Not a lie. Just a message of unwavering love from God. The kind of love not bound by the silly rules we draw around ourselves. Some find that a hard message to absorb."

Ann shrugged and tossed the jacket back, not caring to continue the conversation but understanding that Terry meant no harm.

"Sounds like a lie to me," she responded before walking away from the man.

"We offer food, beds, shelter, and help at the church. It's nearby. You're welcome to come. Lots of kids your age."

Ann snorted. That was the last thing she could ever want. Other kids her age to fear her and ostracize her.

"I'm glad you didn't kill them." Ann stopped abruptly at the words. The same thought echoed in her mind as she wondered where he was going with it. Was he trying to blackmail her with the knowledge of her involvement?

"I'm sure they deserved it. They have quite the reputation around here. Families hug their daughters close at their mention. As written in Exodus, 'but if there is any further injury, then you shall appoint as a penalty life for life, eye for eye, tooth for tooth, and hand for hand.'"

Ann thought about Dave again.

"Someone I loved would be disappointed in me if I had. Not that it matters now. He's dead," she said quietly.

"I'm truly sorry to hear that. But if anything, it matters even more now."

Ann said nothing but waited for him to expand on the thought. "Even if you don't or do believe in heaven and hell, places where souls go, that doesn't take away what they were to you. The people you love form and shape you in their experiences and memories with you."

Terry paused. His gaze looked off farther than distance before continuing. "I had always imagined people as such purely reactive creatures. Simply rolling and flowing around the rocks like water. Things happen, we learn from them, and then we move on. But I think we can be far greater than that if we choose."

Terry's smile was warm and genuine as Ann raised her eyebrows, unimpressed with the flowery words, so he continued.

"I don't believe we exist to simply bounce off the rocks. It may be hard to understand for someone so young, and I don't mean that to be offensive, but I have watched men and women make incredible calls and sacrifices that changed the lives of hundreds and shaped entire communities. What a disservice and a lie to pretend they didn't change the course of their river. I think the same applies for that person who taught you that life is precious, and it requires the stay of the hand sometimes. Through you, your loved one made changes to the river that are already profound, and in you they live."

"He taught me to brush my teeth too, so how come I don't feel closer to him? How come it still feels like my heart and guts have been ripped out?" Ann's voice cracked as the words poured from her broken heart.

"Because regardless of who you are, the world is always going to be a hard place in a few unchangeable respects. We grow so comfortable with the people who love and support us, unable to bear the hole and ache they leave when they are no longer right there. You have to give it time."

Terry's words made sense to Ann but did little to ease the pain and loss she felt right now. "Then maybe with time that won't sound as useless."

She walked away from the priest and wound her way through the alley to a small front yard. She squinted up into the rising sun that only served to contrast her feeling of complete exhaustion. Unfocused and woozy from tiredness, she struggled against her own eyelids that wanted to shut out the world for a needed rest.

Ann spotted a building that seemed to suit her. Most of the windows were intact and the roof still appeared to hold up its responsibility of keeping out the elements. She searched along the wall until she found a small side entrance in the bricks. Scanning back and forth to ensure no one was there to follow her, she dashed to the entryway. It lacked any sort of handle or bar to be pushed. The steel slab appeared flat so as to only be opened from inside. Ann pushed against the door and felt for any movement, but the portal felt as solid as if welded in place.

Might as well be pressing against the brick wall.

Her fingers traced the metal before she closed them into a fist and pressed it against the door.

"Dave . . ." she whispered. Wetness collected in the corners of her eyes as she forced herself to relive all the recent events she would have preferred to forget. Pain swelled in her heart as the loss crashed onto her again. Ann forced Gene's smile into her head and kept it there. The image turned her stomach.

"Asshole." She growled and slammed her fist into the steel door. Ann felt the metal give as easily as clay, and her arm pierced the door. Pulling her hand out of the hole, she examined her fist expecting blood or cuts but there was no sign of any abrasion. Ann looked back at the hole she had punched through the steel with disappointment. The opening was only as large as her fist and the door had stayed in its frame.

"Can't get in through that."

Reaching through, Ann felt for where the handle would be and pushed the door open.

Stepping inside, she stumbled as the darkness overwhelmed her before her eyes could adjust. The morning sun was unable to easily find its way in through the filth-covered windows and stale musty air welcomed her. From the look of faded once-elegant carpet and walls, she guessed it to have been either a hotel or apartment building. The rooms and hallways stood empty of furniture now. After a few paces, she spotted another set of footprints seeming to lead from the front of the building and wandering off toward other areas of the first floor. Ann purposefully went a different route and headed to the nearby stairwell. She clung to the railing for support as she climbed the steps with her aching legs.

Reaching the third floor, she opened the stairwell door and held her breath, listening before stepping out into the hallway. The dust was undisturbed here, which she found comforting. She pushed firmly on the first door she came to, and it grudgingly slid open.

Small and bare, the room confirmed her suspicions that this had been a hotel. There was no longer any bed or other furniture, but the carpet was thick, despite the dust, and the en suite bathroom beckoned her grumbling bowels. She closed the door behind her before sliding the single deadbolt into place. Staring down into the waterless dirt-covered toilet, Ann was just happy the porcelain fixture had been left behind and did what she needed.

She walked over to and slumped down against the wall that directly faced the dead-bolted hallway door. The footprints downstairs made her uneasy. She was determined to be prepared for anyone that made the mistake of harassing her. Exhaustion tugged at the corners of consciousness as she stared at the doorway in the dark. Her head slipped down onto her shoulder as her breathing slowed and sleep found her.

*

Ann's eyes snapped open as she woke. She found herself laid out flat on the old musty carpet. There was a complete darkness now as the morning light that had streamed into the windows was gone and replaced with night. Though it felt like she had only slept for a few fleeting seconds it was obvious several hours had passed.

Rising from the floor, Ann noticed the carpet was damp. Her hair and neck were soaked in cold sweat. She still felt unrested after hours of sleep but stood and stretched anyway. She needed a plan. With shelter temporarily covered, food became a priority.

"No money, no food, dirty clothes . . ." Ann looked down at her ripped and bloodied clothing. Dirty was an understatement.

She couldn't go home. Reappearing into her old life would undoubtedly raise questions she did not want to answer. Besides, what part of her old life was worth it now that Dave was gone?

"None of it. Which makes me homeless." She was determined to try her luck at a local soup kitchen. Hunger lacked the ability to be picky.

Ann unbolted the door and tiptoed her way down the steps to her private entrance. The dust here was in the same state as it had been the day before.

Night had fallen and the moon was high and bright. A few blocks away she could see the divide between worlds clearly. Dead dark towers on one side, illuminated establishments on the other. The lights would have what she needed.

Entering into the glow of Fenny's streetlamps, Ann found her surroundings remarkably similar to what she left behind. The apartments and establishments here were open and lit but still covered in a thick layer of neglect. Not knowing what else to do, Ann started towards Fenny's downtown.

A graying older man digging through a dumpster like he was investigating a bargain bin caught her attention. Glancing up at her, he smiled and gave a nod before returning to his work.

"Excuse me, do you know where there might be a soup kitchen?" she called out.

Without even looking up the man cackled with genuine laughter. "Young miss, do you think if there were any such thing as a soup kitchen in this godforsaken city, I would be doing my eating from a dumpster?"

Ann felt her stomach drop. What little of a plan she had managed now revealed itself to be worthless. "Thank you," she said out of habit. Her walk was much less determined as she continued down the street.

"Now what?" she whispered. An edge of worry settled itself on her thoughts.

Take what you need. You owe them nothing . . .

Again one of her thoughts struck her as discordant but she was unable to pinpoint why.

Ann noticed the cash machine outside the nearby convenience store for the first time. That the thought came before she even knew it was there made her suspicious, but the idea seemed better and better. And she wasn't really harming a particular person. Hunger was a powerful motivator and rationalizer.

"I lived my life according to every rule. I tried so hard for him . . . I tried so hard . . ." she breathed as her resolve broke.

Yes . . .

Walking became sprinting as she closed the distance to the ATM. The power flowed through her with no effort and Ann forced her anger into strength as her hand cut into the thick security steel like birthday cake. Peeling the machine apart, she gasped and her heart leapt when large stacks of twenty dollar bills greeted her. Grabbing at the cash, she felt a real smile for the first time in a long time and sense of relief in the feel of the paper.

They know.

The image of the store clerk flashed behind her eyes and Ann looked up to see the man's panicked face as he spoke into a corded phone. Snatching handfuls of the bills into her pockets she ran back towards the safety of the building she knew. The soft sound of distant sirens grew louder as she ran.

Reaching the building she used as a temporary home, Ann almost entered. Soft sounds of footsteps from deeper in the darkness outside stopped her.

Ducking behind one of the building's outcroppings she waited, hoping the footsteps would stop or change direction.

Instead, they continued steadily in her direction with eerie precision.

"I know you're there. My little buddy has so many sensors in him I can see you four different ways."

Ann's heart caught in her chest as the sound of mechanical whirring could be heard from somewhere above her.

The sirens grew louder.

"I know you might think you're safe out here in the boonies, but Herod is looking for you. You killed Father Gene. He was Herod's guy."

Stunned silent at the mention of Father Gene, Ann tried to gain a hold of the situation. "Who—"

"Who's Herod? Yeah, he's the big shot around here. Best avoided."

The sirens kept growing uncomfortably close. Their piercing wails were like the baying of hunting hounds as they closed in.

"Those cops are crooked and they are coming for you and me. They want me just as badly as you. Well maybe not *as* badly, but we seriously have to leave, and now."

Ann knew she had little choice. She stepped out from behind the wall. His skin and hair were darker than she had expected. Phone in hand, he held it out to her as the large bright screen replayed security camera footage.

Ann recognized herself destroying the ATM.

“I stole this from them when they sent out the call for your arrest. They know what you can do and they aren’t coming to congratulate you,” he warned. “Come with me. I can help.”

Ann nodded.

CHAPTER 12

Onur's mind spun frantically with plans he immediately found flaws in and dismissed while Alton updated him on the situation from a higher vantage point. Their situation was growing more hopeless as he checked his phone's real-time maps. Small red dots on the screen representing police cruisers were closing in from all sides.

"Dammit. They're everywhere. We're going to be surrounded soon."

"Here." Ann reached for her shelter's door.

"Not in there!" he said frantically. Ann stopped and stared at his outburst.

"Sorry. That was rude. My name is Onur, pronounced like the word h-o-n-o-r. Just spelled differently. I was hoping for yours?"

"Oh, Ann."

"Wow, that's . . . plain."

She smiled wryly.

"Oh, man! I mean, it's a beautiful name!" Onur backtracked, realizing he had inadvertently sounded like an ass again. "It's just, I don't know, I guess I was expecting something more . . . exotic." He decided not to delve deeper into now-embarrassing guesses based on childhood comic books.

"Anyway, look, this little home away from home is not a safe house. Some fellas run a meth lab out of the basement. They don't need to come upstairs much with the tunnels that connect to surrounding buildings, but I guarantee you they know you're here now."

"I remember footprints in the dust."

"They would make shit neighbors, I promise."

Onur searched the immediate area and spoke into his phone.

"Alton, am I missing anything?" His phone alerted him to Alton's response.

<Fire escape mechanism can easily be manipulated>

"Do it," he commanded.

"What is that? Who are you talking to?" Ann leaned towards his phone in an attempt to glimpse the screen.

"That is Alton, the first artificial intelligence I ever programmed. And the last AI that I ever coded."

Alton went to work on the fire escape latches. He

methodically triggered the sets of stairs to fall to their next platforms before moving down to the next.

"Why?" she said in awe. "He is amazing."

A robotic chitter sounded from above them like a mixture of laughter and EDM.

"Don't encourage him. His ego is big enough." Onur joked. "He was the last because he kept learning, growing, and developing beyond what I imagined."

The last ladder slid down within reach as Onur finished. Alton flitted down to Onur's shoulder in affection before climbing into the sky again. The cellphone beeped loudly as his screen flashed out a warning.

"Go, go, you first." He hurried her as he signaled up the fire escape stairs. Wasting little time, Ann shot up the ladders. After watching her tear the hardened steel of the ATM apart like wet cardboard, he had not expected what he had found. She was a scared kid running away from terrible people. He followed her up and crouched next to her behind the ledge as an FPD car with flashing lights pulled into the alley. Two officers pulled their weapons and made their way directly towards the entrance of Ann's old shelter.

Must have been the closest cars to her location before the call went out.

"They're just going right in. How did they know?" Ann whispered.

"Word made its way somehow. This whole city has eyes and ears if you're looking. Wait, that's it! Alton, get in the cruiser down there and jack me into the communications system."

After a few stressful moments, <**Connection established**> flared across Onur's screen.

Onur adopted a low gruff voice as he spoke into the mic. "All units, suspect spotted near Swizzler burger and heading south on foot."

Fuck. I didn't say which Swizzler burger.

"Uh, repeat, suspect near Swizzler near 42nd Street. By that pawnshop. It's across from that deli? You know the one." Onur grimaced as finished his train wreck of an announcement and hoped they bought it.

He watched, ecstatic as the small red dots on the screen veered away from their location and sped towards the distant burger joint he had broadcast. The two officers sprinted out from the building with their crackling belt radios alive as they got in their car and sped off.

Ann laughed next to him. "You just screwed them all up."

Onur was less impressed. He knew he had only bought them a bit more time. "Good, because we need to keep Herod out of the loop for as long as possible."

"So who is this Herod guy you keep mentioning?" Ann asked.

Onur had not thought it possible but felt his spirits fell even lower. A long sigh escaped him. This was not the knowledgeable connected ally in the fight against Herod that he had assumed.

"I'm sorry . . . I didn't realize I was supposed to know . . ." Ann began before Onur stopped her.

"No, no, it's not you." He held up his hands in apology. "*I'm* an idiot and sometimes the realization comes at the worst moments. But we can talk about all of that later. For now, follow me down." Onur headed down the ladders again and reached street level. He checked his screen. "Okay . . . Three blocks south and we're in the service area for some of the phone app taxis."

"Will they be able to follow us?"

"Please. None of those idiots is actually a trained police officer. They are just thugs with costumes and badges. And that data is from national companies so it's going to be harder for Herod."

Onur flipped through his screen and picked a ride-hailing application. He ordered pick up as close as possible while making use of a saved stolen credit card number.

"Ok, our ride is on the way. Here we go, run!" They stepped out onto the dark street and sprinted in the cold. The night was alive with sirens in the distance that seemed to be everywhere. Reaching the intersection Onur turned the corner blindly, face buried in his phone as he planned their route.

Tires squealed as a car tried to brake in time before hitting him. Time seemed to slow as Onur looked through the windshield at the driver taking the corner at a dangerous speed. He shut his eyes tight as he braced for impact.

Deafening noise disoriented him as the screech of twisting steel and shattering glass drowned his senses. The asphalt beneath his feet shook and nearly knocked him to the ground.

That's it. I'm dead. Despite the thought, Onur opened his eyes.

The shock of the scene weakened his knees and he fell onto his ass in the street.

Ann clutched the mangled front end of the car as its twisted metal wrapped around her. With the engine leaking fluids onto the road, she shoved the wreck away from herself.

The relief Onur felt was short lived as the hair on the back of his neck stood on end. Something was wrong.

Ann stood in silence, not moving but staring downward like someone trying to remember something before clutching the sides of her head. She screamed but her voice warped and the cry deepened into an inhuman guttural roar. Ann slammed a fist down on the hood of the vehicle with enough force to blow the front tires. Inside, the driver screamed and fumbled with his seatbelt.

At first, Onur thought Ann was simply trying to scare the driver, but now he wasn't so sure that was the case.

"Run you idiot!" Onur's words snapped the driver out of his shocked state. He finally unclicked his seatbelt and kicked the less damaged passenger-side door open before scrambling out of the car. Ann sunk her fingers into the metal and heaved the entire car up with ease as the driver ran for his life. Onur watched in awe as the girl lifted thousands of pounds of automobile as if it were an empty cardboard box.

She moved to throw the vehicle at the driver and crush him.

"Ann!" Onur yelled.

She flinched. The mangled car barely missed the man before fragmenting against the wall. Sparks from grinding metal found leaking gasoline and the flames engulfed the tank. The wreck exploded violently and illuminated the darkness like daylight for a split second.

Ann stared at Onur. Her eyes were black and held no recognition of him. The darkness almost seemed to ooze from her eyes and swirl down like mist.

"Ann? Ann, it's me, Onur. We met like twenty minutes ago and it doesn't bode well for my personality if you already forgot me."

Her eyes returned to normal and recognition softened her gaze. Onur tried to convince himself the blackness must have been a trick of the light. He could tell she was unsteady and confused but knew they had no time for it.

"You good?" he murmured.

Ann nodded slowly as she walked to him.

"Good. Then let's go." He ran.

The sirens seemed to follow them but Onur always took the right turn at the right time to avoid any confrontations. Knowledge was his power. They made their way to the waiting taxi and remained silent for the ride.

Onur still felt exhausted as they entered his building. He led Ann toward the elevator, his legs feeling like solid lead.

"You ok?" Ann asked.

"I'm good," Onur managed as the elevator closed behind them. Leaning against the back of the lift, he took a moment to rest and Ann looked unconvinced.

The elevator doors opened to cold wind whipping the tarp at the end of the hall. Hallway lights flickered weakly as if in danger of blinking away but determined to have someone witness the mold before they went.

"Nice . . . place." Ann stammered.

"The FPD has roomy cells," he said with a grin.

"When you put it that way, yeah, it's perfect."

Onur fumbled through pockets before finally finding his keys and opening the door. Though sparsely furnished to the point of emptiness, a rich deep aroma permeated the apartment. The lovingly crafted stew was still in its Tupperware container.

"Is that food?" she asked with quiet desperation. "I haven't eaten in forever . . ."

"Yeah. All yours." Onur silently told his stomach to shut up as it rioted angrily inside of him.

Bolting the front door, he walked over to his backpack and pulled out a wrapped glass bottle. The dark and gold label was almost as comforting as the heft, which let him know it was full. He kicked off his shoes and pointed towards the bedroom door in the back.

"That is your room. I promise I will never go in it and I don't care what you do." Without another word he walked into the main room and plopped down on the decrepit couch left by previous tenants before taking a pull from the bottle. He listened as she took the Tupperware container into her room.

"It's pretty sad in here," Onur admitted from the couch. "I'll get us fixed up tomorrow. I know a guy."

"There isn't even a bed. But I guess the carpet seems ok," she called out from the room.

"See and that's more than I can say for this couch. It smells awful." Onur made a face and took another swig from the bottle. He turned on his phone and watched a couple of videos as Ann shut the door behind her. He was overall pleased with tonight. Herod had wanted this girl and badly. While not the ally he had been expecting and hoping for, at least she was out of Herod's hands.

Onur's stomach growled again.

"Shut up. These are calories," he muttered and set the bottle down as he got comfortable. "I'll feed you tomorrow."

The distant sounds of the moving and alive city trickled in, almost imperceptible but for the silence of the apartment. Onur nearly nodded off when another sound caught his attention. Muffled sobs came from Ann's room. Onur felt bad for the girl and whatever she had been through but had no idea what to do.

The golden rule, right? Treat others as you want to be treated.

He justified his inaction with the fact that he preferred to be left alone. As the warm whiskey in his stomach began its numbing work he slipped into fitful sleep.

*

Onur woke in an awkward position feeling very sore. *Damn couch!* He groaned as he sat up in the dim apartment and wondered how long he had slept. Looking around it seemed little had changed. Ann's door was still closed and the place remained quiet. He sat back down on the couch and nearly nodded off again when the front door banged open.

Onur stumbled to his feet in terror, thinking Herod had found him. A hoodied Ann stood in the doorway, struggling with bags and a beverage holder. Spotting him she smiled and set the feast down on the table.

"I didn't know what you like, so I sort of got a bit of everything."

"Is that my hoodie your wearing?"

"Oh, yeah, it was on the floor over there. It was cold out there. I hope you don't mind?"

"Boundaries, girl, boundaries. No worries, we'll get you your own," he complained before spotting the orange liquid in one of the clear cups.

"Is that orange juice?" He breathed.

"Yeah, they fresh squeeze apparently. That place was awesome! Its four blocks down and I was walking past when I smelled amazing hazelnut coffee." She talked quickly and was breathless with excitement from her morning walk in the city.

Onur grabbed the juice and popped off the top before taking a deep gulp. He closed his eyes with a pleased sigh.

"You rock. So much," he said earnestly before digging through the bags of food. Spotting an egg-and-bacon bagel sandwich, he tore into it.

Onur ambled to the couch while alternating between sips of juice and bites of food as he regained speaking terms with his stomach.

Ann sat next to him on the couch with coffee but her face pinched as the furniture's odor reached her. She stood up and settled herself on the carpet with a bite of her bagel.

"Yeah, I don't blame you," he agreed. They ate in silence before Onur spoke up.

"I don't recommend spending too much more of that money."

"You seem to be enjoying breakfast," Ann quipped. "Should I be expecting an unwanted lesson on saving?"

Onur chuckled.

"It's not that. Banks can trace their bills with the serial numbers. Make a big enough purchase somewhere with their stolen money and they will check security footage to glean all sorts of clever information on finding you."

Ann grew thoughtful.

"Also, don't sweat the furniture and living arrangements. Someone owes me."

"Herod?" Ann questioned.

Onur stared at her and realized she spoke earnestly, ignorant of the dangerous name and its connotations. "How much do you know about all this, Ann? What do you know about the people trying to hunt you down?"

She took a deep breath. The smile and joy were gone from her face. "I have no idea what happened or why." She spoke softly as she looked down at her coffee. "I used to live at the placement center before my social worker, Dave, took me in and adopted me. Well, not officially, but he kept trying."

Onur began working his phone.

"I lived with him ever since, at least until three days ago. Father Gene told me he killed him." Ann grew quiet.

"What happened?"

"We were in the city and these two guys grabbed us." Her voice wavered. Onur gave her a few moments.

"Did one of the guys kinda look like a grizzly bear wearing human clothes?"

Ann laughed at the mental image and nodded yes.

"That's Norman all right." He assumed the other man to be Nick.

"You know him?"

"They worked for Gene. Norman was his muscle. Though somewhat reluctant muscle from what I've heard. Did you know Father Gene at all before this?"

"No." She thought. "Well, he said he first met me when I was at the placement center, but I don't remember that. Maybe it happened when I was really young."

Looking down at his phone Onur gave a long low whistle. "And it looks like he tried to adopt you no fewer than thirty-three times. That's a little excessive."

Ann gasped as the pieces added up.

"That's what he meant when he said, 'despite Dave's attempts' to protect me from him."

"Good guy then, because Father Gene is the kind of awful that would make sex offenders move from a neighborhood. Not that anyone in his damn cult would admit anything about the real asshole he is."

Onur smiled.

"I mean *was*. He is a dead asshole at least."

Ann didn't seem to share his enthusiasm.

"How did he bite it?"

"I don't remember. But I think I ripped his throat out," Ann whispered.

Awkward silence filled the room as Onur digested her words.

Ann looked at him strangely. "I thought you would ask me the question everyone else does. What am I? How do I do those things?"

Onur stopped eating.

"I wasn't going to press you for answers you didn't want to give. But by all means, if you want to share, I'll listen."

"I don't know."

He wasn't sure if that had been her complete thought. "Like, you don't know if you can trust me with your secret?"

She shook her head. "No. Like I don't know how or why that stuff happens to me."

At that moment, Alton flitted in through the open window and buzzed around the room before landing on Onur.

"Where was he?" she asked in surprise.

"Scanning and watching to make sure we don't get any surprise visitors."

Waving a finger at the small robot, she called out to Alton as though he were a puppy. The AI creation flitted and buzzed around her playfully and landed on her shoulder.

What the hell happened to my life? He had been a

loner getting by with himself and no one to hold him down or be responsible for. In one night, that had all changed. Onur felt responsible for this girl and was beginning to care for her.

"Okay," he said with a sigh before taking another satisfying swig of orange juice. "Let me fill you in on Herod."

CHAPTER 13

Nius's time in the city had honed his abilities and he touched down gently on a jutting gargoyle. He flexed his legs and leapt, windows and brick blurring past as he rushed upwards onto the roof. He had been on his way back to Terry's church but now slumped down the concrete lip in exhaustion until he was seated.

The sleepless nights were growing longer as Nius found himself more and more occupied with the helpless of the city. Yawning in the bright morning light, he found himself relieved that dusk was still so many hours away. He felt stretched thin and tired, and night was the worst.

Crime seemed to permeate every block of the city but for the massive downtown. Fenicia's criminals seemed to be mostly the poor fighting among themselves for what little scraps there were. Crime seemed to only happen in the worse-off areas and it didn't make sense to Nius when there was a downtown that practically screamed of money and well-to-do tourists.

That was, until he had made the mistake of venturing near the bright, glamorous downtown. A heavy police presence answered his question as to why the gangs didn't roam there.

In the rest of the city, the crime was predictable but easily stopped. That wasn't the case at night, however.

Always the screams came first. Armed and masked men worked with an eerie calm and practiced quiet as they stormed sleeping homes to take captives. Nius didn't know who was doing it or why, but he realized soon, it went higher up than he'd first suspected.

Twice now, the FPD arrived, greeting and freeing these milita types that Nius had managed to bind for arrest. His heart had dropped into his stomach like a stone.

If it's corruption, just how high does it go? Why does the FPD arrest and stop petty crime but turn a blind eye to what seem to be human traffickers? What is happening in this city?

The churning unease deep inside him would not cease, adding to the already plentiful doubts and fears that he had on his first day in Fenny. The loss of his backpack, with his only possessions and the money

Cheryl had given him, was at least something he could fix. He hoped against hope it would still be there.

On the roof, Nius moved away from the busy street to the side that faced the alley before dropping down unseen. Stepping out onto the main street he tried to appear nonchalant, walking inconspicuously and keeping his gaze forward.

He took the church's steps three at a time, reaching for the heavy wooden door. It was cracked and splintered from the FPD officers forcing their way in. He ran his fingers over the damage to the beautiful carved wood, unable to shake the feeling that this was completely his fault.

The church was quiet and empty. He thought better of calling out to anyone and instead moved towards Terry's office.

With the majority of the lights in the church either off or broken in the raid, it was surprising to see a soft glow coming through the frosted office window.

Why does this feel like a trap? A sense of calm pulled him towards Terry's door, no internal warning or unease as he reached for the knob.

Terry sat alone at his desk, deep in thought as Nius slipped the door open. Oblivious to the interruption, the priest continued to stare at his hands as they fidgeted in the eerie silence.

Nius cleared his throat to get Terry's attention.

Terry raised his head, suspicious eyes becoming a happy smile as he confirmed the young man's face.

"Um . . . hi?"

"I was hoping you would come back. Well, maybe a little more than hoping," Terry said with a chuckle as he glanced over at the large traveling pack in the corner of the room.

"My bag!" Nius breathed in relief as he hopped over, digging through it. "And the money! It's still here!" he exclaimed. He realized he was implying he was surprised that Father Terry had not robbed him.

"I meant, instead of . . . I thought . . . I dropped it. Off a boat."

Terry's grin only grew larger.

"Don't you worry about me, kid. You won't hurt my feelings." He leaned forward. "But you—we need to talk about you."

Something about the conversation reminded Nius of those he had shared with Cheryl. He wondered what on earth the man had to say to him. Rising to his feet, Terry stepped around the desk. Nius tensed but did not move as the towering man walked right up to him. With no warning, Terry wrapped his arms around Nius. The priest smelled of fresh-cut lumber and baked bread. The aroma calmed Nius as he was pulled into a bear hug.

After a few long seconds, Terry finally let go, taking a step back as he beamed at Nius.

"I don't think you really understand what you are doing," the large man said to him knowingly. "In the city, I mean."

"I completely agree," Nius muttered sarcastically as his eyes shifted downward. "I don't understand the police or why they behave like they do. I don't understand the city and what's going on. Just about the only thing I do understand, is how little I actually understand."

The smile had not left Terry's face as he waited for Nius to finish.

"Did anyone get hurt when I ran?" Nius asked, nearly whispering the question in fear of the response.

"You can rest easy." Terry assured him, "No one was hurt when you left. But I hear you have been busy since that night."

"Mostly running from the authorities."

The priest laughed but shook his head in disagreement with the word. "No, not authorities. Authority implies we have given them the right to enforce justice for us, and no one who lives and works in this city had any say in the matter."

"What's happening then? Who are the masked men taking people in the middle of the night at gunpoint?

Why do the police ignore them and everything else outside of downtown?"

"Those are answers I don't have. Truthfully, you may know more than I do about everything happening now."

Nius felt dwindling hope fade altogether. He had thought Terry would be able to tell him everything.

Terry must have seen his deflation. He spoke up again. "But I will still tell you what I do know. I only ask that you give me details on what you saw. I know you saved over fifteen people from God knows what."

"Fair enough, what do you want to know?"

"Whatever seems important," Terry replied. "And even things that won't seem so important to you, but are to me."

Nius nodded his understanding.

"First off, what kinds of guns did they carry? Did you manage to catch any makes or models?"

"I never saw anything like them. They almost seem to be custom made."

Terry thought on this answer for a few moments and each passing second seemed to make the man more uneasy.

"Did they act randomly? Was it just a bunch of guys grabbing people and taking them?"

Nius was surprised at the question as he thought

about it. It was almost as if Terry expected the answers before he even asked the questions. "No, they were definitely coordinated. They moved like a team, surrounding me when I interrupted them, and reacting like a single unit. I probably would have noticed more if they hadn't been trying to kill me."

"Did you manage to follow any of the vehicles and see where the people are being taken?"

Nius made a face. "Tried to. I think they figured out what I was doing because a small group split off to come back for me while the others kept going. After that, I was mostly running."

If Terry had been pondering before, he was completely lost in his thoughts now, sitting still as if carved from steel. Nius gave the large man time to collect his thoughts. The lull stretched on, however, and an antsy Nius finally urged the conversation forward.

"They didn't talk at all either—at least I didn't hear them. No shouting, no yelling codes or maneuvers. They seemed to stay completely silent; I still don't know how they communicated and worked so well."

Terry sighed, rubbing his eyes and temples.

"Throat microphones," he replied. "You wear the collar around your neck and it can pick up even the tiniest whisper. You could be strapped to a speeding motorcycle with the wind whipping past you and I would hear you clear as a bell. Between those, and hands signals, you wouldn't have heard much."

Terry's explanation made sense to Nius. After all, the armed kidnappers had been geared to the teeth with equipment and weapons. The explanation of their tactics made sense too.

"Now I'll tell you what I know. The FPD has not been able to call itself a police department since the old police chief Jim Mallon disappeared."

Terry leaned back in the chair. "Honestly, things had been getting worse for years. I can't remember exactly when the decline started. Looking back, it feels like it happened overnight, but really it was gradual—years in the making. When Jim disappeared, though, things went from bad to awful. I can honestly say we fear for our lives. The FPD are not so much officers as they are thuggish bodyguards for those who can afford the influence. They are dangerous and not on our side, kid, not a one of 'em. Maybe there were a few good, honest guys working with Jim, but I am sure after he disappeared, they were forced to either crook up or die."

Nius sat and absorbed as much as he could, his desperately incomplete picture of Fenny filling in a bit.

"And the G.I. Just-Get-In-The-Truck guys?"

"That started the night you left here. I had heard snippets, rumors. But then the ones you saved came here, afraid to go home again. They told me what they could, but they didn't know half of the information you do."

Nius looked around, the quiet and empty church stirring so many questions. Terry answered them before Nius could ask.

"We spread out. Moved underground, so to speak, hiding. I won't say where. Don't take offense, there is not a soul on earth I would trust with all of that unnecessary information." Changing the subject away from those in his protection, the priest turned the conversation back towards Nius.

"They left a stake-out for you that night, hoping you would come back. They only stayed one night, though, and then left in a hurry, like something more important got their attention," Terry said cryptically.

What few answers Nius managed to find here showed him how ignorant he was of the situation. The lack of sleep and food coupled with the lack of answers had begun to gnaw at him.

"I'm new here, so I get why I don't really know much. But you're not telling me all that much more and you live here."

He left it at that, not really sure how to continue.

"We aren't ignorant out of a desire to be, kid. Whatever those politicians and moneymen do at the top rung of society, they make damn sure we don't see. If you have any other questions, I will always tell you everything I know. But I am sorry and I will tell you now, it is not going to be much. There are, however, people out there who I am sure know all the power players and what is going on in much more detail than I ever will. But we are just trying to get by, survive and raise families, because we were the unlucky ones who couldn't and can't get out."

Terry's face lit up, a happiness that was completely at odds with the subject matter he spoke of.

"Until you." He grinned. "You saved all those people, yes, but you have done so much more than that. People don't speak in hushed whispers anymore, as if the walls themselves will come alive and kill them. Hope isn't a concept so distant that they have never felt its warmth. They talk about you and how you put your life on the line for them—THEM! The nothings of the world. You might feel overwhelmed, like you're trying to push back the sea with a paddle. But know this: you are bringing change, desperately needed change."

Nius remained silent, taken aback and unsure of what to say until his frustrations reared their head. "That's really nice. I'm glad, I really am, but you seem to have this picture of a powerful, in-control savior that knows what he is doing."

"Do we? You don't think I see the dumb scared kid in front of me?"

"Uh . . . thanks?"

The advice and conversation were reminiscent of his childhood. He felt himself ache for Cheryl and Mona, to feel the cabin's wooden floors under his feet and breathe the forest air into his lungs.

"People have cared with all their hearts and souls, given themselves whole to the fight and failed, especially Jim." Terry looked at him earnestly and Nius realized he, too, had begun to hope. "However, where they failed, I feel you will not. I get the feeling you will see your way through."

Nius stared at the floor as he tensed, hoping to avoid any discussion of his powers. That was another thing he didn't understand; his abilities and the limits of his protection were easily reached in the dangerous city. Though already in the city for a few days, he seemed to be procrastinating on the entire point of his trip to Fenny.

"I won't press you about that, I promise. But I would like to know your name."

Nius relaxed a bit. "Nius. Well, Munius. Nius for short."

Terry sat thoughtfully for a few moments, rolling the name around in his head. "Munius? The Egyptian name for Moses? The prophet who used supernatural powers given by God to free his people?"

"My . . . mom gave me the name. She was a nun. She left the convent. Then we moved to the woods." Nius left it at that, rising to leave with bag in hand now that Terry had told him everything he knew.

"You are just full of surprises. You know your scripture and your mom was a nun, so I know you have your faith in order. Where will you go now?"

Nius nearly flinched as he remembered Cheryl and his conflicted thoughts on that, the truth much muddier. "I don't know."

"Well, before you go wherever that is, I have one last thing to tell you." Terry spoke hesitantly. "I think there is someone else out there—another person like you."

Nius froze.

"I saw her the other day. Not a bad person, but seemed lost. She seemed . . . powerful, but angry."

He had never heard of anyone else that might be like him. He said nothing, wondering what else Terry might reveal.

"Anyway, stay safe, Nius, and listen to yourself. You have a lot of the answers you need inside."

Don't I wish . . .

"And remember, I'm always here if you need. Just

make sure you don't have company following you first," Terry said, leaving it at that.

Nius nodded and left through the church's back entrance, feeling a little more informed but just as adrift and lost. Patting his large bag brought a small measure of relief; the money and belongings comforted him in such a dangerous and unforgiving city.

The priest had given him a lot to think about, his hopelessness pepped by Terry's words of encouragement. Now he needed some breakfast.

CHAPTER 14

Dry stinging air caused Herod to cough and gag. Heat robbed his mouth and throat of moisture. Shielding his eyes against the red light that covered the city, he felt the gnawing worry that haunted him ceaselessly. His footsteps felt leaden.

Light snow fell over him but there was no chill to the flakes. Holding out his hand, he caught it, but looking closer, he realized it was falling ash. Herod lifted his gaze and watched as buildings wept streams of sand. The bricks powdered to ash as their strength gave way. Reaching down he clutched a handful of the blackened dust and watched it run through the gaps in his fingers.

From the heap of ash an arm shot up. It grabbed Herod's ankle with unshakable strength. Herod cried out in fear as other arms punched through the concrete and blacktop. They were followed by more and more as the hands stretched on as far as he could see. His desperate screams grew muffled as the thick, choking ash closed in around him, strangling him into silence as the arms clutched and clawed at his body.

He woke screaming into the darkness, wrestling with sweat-soaked sheets that clung to him. Herod breathed in deeply through his nose and exhaled out his mouth to calm himself. Reaching up, he pressed near his neck. Relief flooded back as his fingertips found the small GPS panic button implanted under his skin.

The nightmare faded as he sat on the edge of the bed. Every moment in the darkness stole more and more details until only vague outlines remained. He ran to a drawer across the room and hurriedly dug for a pen and paper to jot down what little he remembered. Never much for dream journals or interpretations, Herod felt silly jotting it down, yet on some level he was compelled to. He wanted every detail he recalled recorded, but they too slipped through his fingers.

Is it left to me to stop these inhuman creatures and save us from destruction?

His wet nightclothes stuck clammily to his skin. Herod unbuttoned his silk shirt top and let it fall to the floor as he stepped out of his soft pajama leggings. He took a moment in the cool air to let it soothe his body after the oppressive heat of his dream.

Nightmare fading, the previous day's events

returned to his thoughts, and with them the displeasure of humiliation and self-doubt. His calm, cool exterior had begun to show signs of cracking in front of his men.

Charlie seemed fully on board and had promised a prototype in a matter of days. He had not been lying. Charlie just failed to specify whose prototype he had finished.

Even Herod had to admit the weapon was incredible. The alloy was Charlie's life's work and it appeared to reflect light in odd and colorful directions. Sleek lines and a simple but beautiful build made Herod fall in love with the weapon, until he realized what he was looking at. It would provide no pulses of energy, no beams of destructive light, no shredding of modern military armor built to stop bullets. Charlie had built something entirely different.

"Each projectile round is capable of penetrating through a half foot of hardened steel; there is nothing like it in existence!" Charlie had tried to explain angrily. He had looked dumbfounded that Herod would be upset.

"And how much per gun, Charlie? Better yet, how much per bullet?"

Charlie was evasive and gave no real answer. Herod had learned the truth that between smelting the alloy and manufacturing it to precise specifications, each rifle would cost nearly half a million. The specialized rounds it fired would cost hundreds per bullet. It was utterly unfeasible to arm all his men with such weapon. He would deal with Charlie soon enough.

Herod could almost feel their eyes. Hard-earned respect and fear becoming questions and subterfuge. He would not tolerate it, as Charlie would learn.

"Just a miscalculation, an underestimation."

Mistakes. He seemed to be making so many of them now.

Closing his eyes, Herod let the images of Nius replay in his head. Bullets seemed to slide around him as they followed some unknown path and the boy remained unscathed.

He had cared little for what FPD officers described as a leaping, running maniac. They had claimed he dodged their bullets, but Herod had assumed it was a fabricated story to cover for their awful marksmanship. Had he known what the boy was truly capable of, he would have instead approached with gifts and charm. That opportunity was surely gone now.

Well, if he views the FPD in bad light, then I simply have to remain separate from them. And keep him away from that annoying hacker.

As for Ann, he had already lost that battle to the hacker. His team had arrived at the torn ATM too late it seemed. The parasite clung to his networks like a fat grub sucking life from tree roots and must have intercepted. In hindsight, it was easy to piece together the timeline. Some of his methamphetamine producers reported a one-night squatter in the hotel they used. The homeless people in the area knew better than to interfere, and they avoided such places. The destroyed ATM was mere blocks away from the hotel, and it was clear now the girl had been running blind and helpless.

Until that smug prick got involved . . . But why should he care?

Afterwards, it had not been difficult to trace the break in his network security. The flaw was quickly patched but the damage was already done, as was always the case with the hacker. Even Herod knew he played a losing game of cat and mouse when it came to his IT security team. His educated and highly paid technicians could only close the holes the young man showed them.

"I refuse to let this be how I come crashing down."

Herod went to his bedside table, picked up his cellphone and dialed his installed chief of police.

"There are a few things I need to—"

"I hate to interrupt you, sir. We think we have a lead on the male kid and are tracking him as best we can from a distance."

Any anger or resentment at being quieted was gone.

"I want him followed. No more hourly updates—just a daily report of where he goes and

what he does."

"It's not that simple with this kid and how he moves, but we'll do our best."

"Do not forget the girl. I want her captured alive."

"But, sir . . . She's with the hacker now. It's going to be impossible."

"Then we wait, or we bait. There is something in this city that the asshole wants or he would have left by now. And I think I know what it is. Remember, do not move on the boy. I will capture him myself."

"How will you capture the kid without FPD support? He has beaten down squads singlehandedly."

"You need to think in multiple dimensions." Herod hung up the call with renewed hope.

He knew now with little doubt that he could not approach this young man as the powerful and in-control figurehead that he had built over the years. Herod would need to distance himself from the FPD and from the criminal empire he had spent his whole life creating. From what he had seen of those two kids, they could spread his control far beyond Fenicia.

And if I don't, these two will likely end our world.

Sitting in his still office, Herod watched the sun

creep over the horizon and chase the darkness from the streets. He was unable to remember the last time he had done so. An early riser, he had been present for countless sunrises, but never settled in for the express purpose of watching the day's birth. The glittering gem of downtown rolled on before him.

His eyes followed the curves and sharp colors of the city but stopped at the borders he preferred to ignore. Tremendous skyscrapers dotted the landscape past where the current city limits stood, some much larger than anything currently in use. They stood as giant relics of a time past when everyone in the city prospered and Fenicia pressed against her boundaries. They now stood gray, dead, and empty.

He had watched as those abandoned areas had spread and grown under his grip on the city. He had always imagined his leadership would mean wealth and prosperity like Fenicia had never known. It had stung to see that his control triggered a massive decline. Despite his best efforts to focus the wealth of the city into a few capable families, the city had continued dying. The only thing that had kept the breath of life in downtown Fenicia had been its wealthy citizens. It was a welcome change for the rich who now saw the city as their own private living area that catered to their wants and needs. It had been difficult coming to the realization that his dreams of ruling had been warped and twisted by necessity, but fate had shown him the answer.

"Those two could change everything . . ." he whispered.

A sharp knock on the office door shook him from his thoughts. "Yes?" he asked through the intercom system beside the door, wary even in his own home.

"Donovan Olevot is here to see you."

"I have nothing scheduled with him, what the hell does he want?"

"I have no idea, but he is very certain of himself today. He has eight men with him; they brushed me aside and forced their way into the den. They are, for the most part, staying put at the urging of your private security team. Though one or two seem to have broken from the pack. They outnumber your suite security but if you request, I'll call for additional backup."

"With what my team is armed with, it's unnecessary. I'll go see them now." Herod heaved open the door and stepped past the assistant.

"Sir, would you prefer to change into something more professional?" The assistant eyed his silk pajamas.

"They are in my home unannounced in the early morning. What are they to expect? For me to panic myself into a suit to impress them?"

Herod strode into his own den and eyed the jumble of Donovan Olevot's bodyguards before heading straight for Olevot himself. Dressed in an impeccable white suit, the large blond man lounged on Herod's leather couch and smirked at the sleeping wear.

"I don't even warrant putting on pants?"

"I'm not sure how much clearer your answer could be." Herod wasted no pleasantries or even tolerance on the interruption. "If you were to ask me, the moneybags of this city spend far too much time and energy strutting like peacocks with their eyes always on the feathers of others, wondering if they are more expensive and shiny. I disagree with the saying that the clothes make the man. After all, your beautiful expensive suit is currently being worn by the spoiled, pretentious offspring of a much greater man."

Donovan's ruddy cheeks grew bright red as his jaw clenched. He rose rapidly from his sitting position trying to tower over the shorter Herod. The sudden movement brought unease to the room as Herod's men shuffled and trained their weapons on the man. Donovan stared down hard at him but Herod smirked and easily matched the glare until Donovan backed down.

"You wouldn't be stupid enough to kill me," Donovan spat, trying to disguise his surrender.

"And you shouldn't be stupid enough to force your

way into my home armed and unannounced. Yet here you are."

"My father would—"

"For the sake of your own self-respect, please stop. You will not be taken seriously by me as long as you continue trying to get by in this city on Manfred's name."

Donovan sneered at Herod but remained quiet. He flopped down again on the sofa, spreading his arms across the back of it trying to mimic possession and comfort, and tried another tack. "Sounds to me like you just have daddy issues. Did you not have a father?"

"Are you offering to be my therapist? Is that why you are here this morning, to extend your services? I must decline."

Looking to the head of his security Herod nodded towards the door.

"Get him out of here." His security team closed in around Donovan and his men while barking directions and orders urging them towards the exit.

"They want to know what's happening, Herod. They want to be informed!" Donovan shouted to him as Herod walked away, referring to the wealthy families of the city.

"Then they can contact me directly."

"Bullshit, how many calls have you ignored? They know you're dodging them!"

Herod faced him and held up a hand to stop his guards.

"And you expect me to believe the wealthy families of Fenny have appointed you as their mouthpiece?"

"I'm the only one who would come. There are explosions in the streets, your officers swarming everywhere with RPGs and high-powered weapons. Rumors of who knows what running around. Is this the norm now? Because it's not what we paid for!"

"Remind me again what you paid for. Please, refresh my memory on your place in all this."

Donovan became unsure and stumbled over his words. He had no retort to Herod's honest question. He had been a child when the takeover of Fenicia had begun. Donovan's father Manfred Olevot had been instrumental in Herod's success as the installed head of internal affairs. After turning the police force for Herod, Manfred retired to the other side of the planet to enjoy his spoils. But his son seemed to be just another entitled power-hungry child given everything he had ever wanted.

"I'm not here for anyone and I don't speak for anyone. But there are angry whispers out there wanting to know what's happening and what you're doing about it. They deserve—"

"They deserve?" Herod repeated it to himself as

though the words were disgusting in his mouth. If he had matched Donovan's gaze before, his look now cowed the young man, who pulled his outstretched relaxed arms in toward his body nervously.

"What do those decadent assholes deserve? I found them chained to the system when I arrived. Their money bought parks and schools in places they wouldn't step foot in. They were bound by rules and laws meant for the lesser." He paused for a moment as he recalled his struggle.

"I was the one who bled, I was the one who plotted and executed, I was the only one to make who I am."

Donovan stayed silent.

"Get him the fuck out of my home for his father's sake, before I change my goddamn mind," Herod growled before heading deeper into his penthouse. "Fenny's so-called upper crust will get their answers when I see fit."

Herod sighed as he settled himself into the office chair once again. Donovan Olevot's words contained undeniable kernels of truth. The city's richest citizens were essential to the continued operation of downtown Fenny as a desired tourist destination for the wealthy.

The families had agreed to create a bastion of wealth and power with the promise of Herod's backing and changes to laws. Herod viewed the poor as dirtying his streets and stymieing his efforts to create a great society.

Herod strode over to his office door, slamming it shut against the world. He had much to plan.

CHAPTER 15

The late night had most of the residents either sleeping or searching for the elusive state of mind. Traffic flowed on the never-still streets of Fenicia but the distant sounds were ignored by Onur as he reclined on a large comfortable couch. He was bathed in the glow of their flat screen television as he watched a terrible B movie and checked his phone. His everything-supplying friend Rodne had come through, though it was all likely stolen.

Most of his attention was focused on the screen of his phone, but a small chuckle escaped him as the movie's cheap monster appeared on screen stumbling awkwardly.

His attention switched back and he watched the data scroll past. He had been hoping for further information or more sightings on the strange happenings around Fenicia. He normally had one ear to the ground about everything going on, but he had been slacking the last few days. Instead, he had done his best to accommodate his unexpected roommate.

He had at first assumed the rumors of someone with superhuman abilities circulating online were about Ann and had tried to bury them. But looking closer, he realized the locations and claims did not match up with anything she had done or anywhere she had been.

Someone is running around doing parkour off skyscrapers and dodging Herod's gunships, but it's not Ann. She was with me when this was supposed to have happened. So if it's not her, then who the hell? In the darkness, a chill ran down his spine as he remembered what she could do. These new unsubstantiated reports claimed such extraordinary events that Onur would have scoffed if he had read them just a few days ago.

It's funny how experience changes things. Was there perhaps more of the crazy and impossible out in the world than he had ever thought?

"What am I doing?" he muttered, knowing full well he was procrastinating. "I have no idea where Jim's family is and now I'm looking for boogeymen and urban legends." His search for the location of Jim's wife and daughter was a complete dead end. Herod had learned from Onur's weaknesses and adjusted. General communications still used the internet, but any vital information was now kept under closed-wired local systems.

Imagine having the money to have city workers build your own LAN and lay the wire and guard it. With no connections to the outside world there were no ways in for the brilliant hacker. If he wanted access to that information now, he'd have to have access to a machine on Herod's private network. And those machines were only in a few specific places. Banks and businesses Herod had direct control over. With the huge increase in security at those places, getting in was an impossible suicidal waste of thought.

Unless I can somehow get past dozens of beefed-up guys swinging around assault rifles. And manage not to get shot long enough to access the network with no usernames or passwords. And of course make it out again. Preferably not in a Ziplock baggie.

Regardless of how impossible it seemed, Onur still couldn't stop floating the idea as he drowned in guilt. His promise to Jim was eating away at him. It had been over a week and what awful horrors were his wife and daughter enduring while Onur sat on his comfortable couch?

Reaching for the small side table, he brought the weed vape to his lips, breathing in warm aromatic vapor and holding it in before succumbing to a coughing fit. Warm tingles spread through his body and Onur felt his tense muscles relax.

While normally something of an alcoholic, Onur was surprised at how little liquor he had been downing these last few days. But ever since Ann had moved in, things had been different and though Onur would never admit it, the changes had been positive for the two. But his love of the marijuana was going to be lifelong.

The movie gave him another laugh as the leading lady gave a fake scream and the badly made monster costume waddled towards her.

A much louder blood curdling scream rent the night and Onur's heart nearly jumped out of his chest as he clambered to his feet. The cry had come from Ann's room.

Her night terrors were a regular thing now. Onur worried for her because nightmares and insomnia were problems he had dealt with and he didn't wish them on anyone else. Well . . . maybe Herod.

Day by day, Ann was speaking less and less and growing more withdrawn from Onur. This was one reason he had not broached the subject of action against Herod. He worried he might drive her off if it seemed he simply wanted her abilities. After all, what really separated him from Herod if he wanted to use her only for her powers?

You would be lying if you weren't also a little scared of whatever is going on with her. He remembered her actions and the look in her eyes that night. She remembered none of it, so what was he supposed to make of that?

Settling back down on the couch, he stuck to his selfish promise not to bother her in her room and let the quiet in the apartment resume. Guilt and conscience crept up on him, prodding and pressing: *why didn't he check on Ann?*

Yeah. Run into the room with the terrified girl who can punch your teeth *down* into your stomach. Smart.

But that wasn't really it. He was just scared of feeling for her. Scared of feeling for anyone else, because look what it had gotten him.

"Probably a good idea then to not care," he muttered aloud to no one.

But it's too late and you know it. He sighed at the truth.

"I should drown you in whiskey again," he complained to his conscience.

Ann's door creaked open. She stood in the open doorway and looked around the apartment. Her gaze landed on Onur as he watched his movie. After what seemed like minutes, she took a few steps toward him and stood next to the couch watching the screen. Not wanting to reveal he had heard her nightmare screams, Onur pretended to be oblivious.

"Still awake?" she asked, nervous eyes flicking back from the TV to him. He made a point of removing his earbuds, hoping she would take it as a sign he had not heard her.

"Oh yeah. Sleep and I don't get along too well."

"I've seen you sleep for hours."

"Ah. You see that is an easy mistake to make but what you saw was passed out. Big difference," he kidded, drawing a smile from her.

"Do you mind if I watch with you?"

"Not at all. Have a seat." He nodded towards the free spot on the couch. To have her leave her room and join him was a welcome change.

"What are you watching?" she asked quietly.

"Terror time in the dark lagoon. Awful, terrible movie. Just, wow. Look, you can see the idiot's zipper down the back." He laughed as he pointed out the monster's obvious costume opening.

Ann snickered as she watched the movie monster's mask swelling and shrinking as the actor inside struggled to breathe.

"If it's so bad why are you watching it?"

"Are you kidding me? Sometimes terrible movies are the best. In fact, sometimes an awful movie can be funnier than a good comedy." Both began laughing again as the fake creature stumbled over the set and nearly fell.

"So what brings you out here tonight?"

Ann looked down uncomfortably. Onur wondered if maybe even that comment was too much too fast.

"You really didn't hear?"

Without skipping a beat, Onur easily lied in the hopes it would make her feel better. "Hear what? Another nightmare? I didn't hear anything. Ear buds." He held out the two ear buds.

Accepting the explanation, Ann seemed relieved. "I had another dream. They are getting worse."

"You never had this problem before?"

Ann shook her head.

"I have had some problems with nightmares since I was a kid, but never like this and never this bad. It feels different now . . . They always used to feel so far away when I was little. Like something I was watching on the other side of the street. They didn't happen that often but now . . ."

"You can't seem to go a night," Onur finished for her.

Ann nodded before growing quiet.

"And it all stems from this feeling?"

It seemed this was the needed trigger to get Ann

going because the girl's eyes grew wider as she tried to find a way to describe everything to him.

"It is like anger. It's rage. But also recognition. Like I see someone I knew years ago, but I don't. These feelings don't feel like mine . . . I'm sorry this probably sounds so stupid." Ann fumbled her words, embarrassed.

"No," Onur said loudly. "It's not stupid and it's not weird. I have seen you throw a car farther than I can throw . . . well, anything. Everything you feel and everything you see and dream could mean so much more for someone like you. And I know you must have grown up wishing for normality, but why? What I saw was amazing!"

Ann smiled shyly.

Onur went on. "But don't answer that because I know why. It must have been awful trying to fit in, I get it. Kids can be cruel. But this is the real life and you, Ann, are amazing. Embrace it and live it without shame because you are one in a billion. You can do whatever you want!"

She sat and thought as Onur wrestled with himself internally. This was the perfect time to try and he could not have planned it better.

"Anyway, I have some really worrisome stuff to deal with right now." He sighed and just as he had hoped, Ann peered at him curiously.

"What's that?" she asked.

"You're not the only one Herod and Gene had their eyes on." He knew Ann would be interested at the mention of Gene. "I made a promise to Jim when I tried to break him out. When they took him, they also took his wife and daughter.

"I have been searching and digging for where Herod might be holding them, but it's no use. The only way to find out where they are is to get into his closed network and that's damn-near impossible."

"The things that they must be going through . . . I can remember Gene bragging about his brothels and what would happen to me," Ann said softly.

Onur had been taking a pull from his vaporizer when her words hit him. He gasped while inhaling the weed vapor, triggering a coughing fit as he rolled around on the couch.

"Are you ok?" Ann couldn't help but ask.

"*Fine, great even!*" Onur gasped through coughs and tear-filled red eyes, "You gave me a new lead!" He beamed at her as the coughing fit subsided. He began tapping at his phone, looking again at Herod's closed network.

"There are scattered access consoles throughout the city, but only in important places that need them. Herod must be using his human trafficking network and brothels to keep Jim's family off the grid and secure. There are dozens of brothels operating in Fenny and they could be in any one of them, but look here." He held his phone's screen toward Ann and pointed. "Only these four communicate with Herod's internal network. The rest just deposit and report their earnings via the regular network. If I can just get into one of those four, looking like a regular customer, I might be able to find where they are keeping Jim's family."

Ann shifted on the couch until she was facing him.

"I want to help."

"I don't know, Ann. This is not going to be easy. We are both insane and in danger if we go through with this. I don't think I can ask that of you."

"Then think of it as me forcing you to accept my help—so shut up and too bad. I'm not doing this for you. I was in that awful room under Gene's house, so I know what happens to the girls they take. I want to help. Didn't you just say I can do whatever I want? I'm sick of sitting around and I'm sick of doing nothing except living day to day scared of my own nightmares."

Onur watched as she spoke and her eyes grew dark.

"But most of all, I'm so sick of the people who did all this. I hate that they are fine and that they go about their lives like nothing happened. I hate that they tore us apart and thought nothing of it. They killed Dave and it meant nothing to them."

Black mist began flowing like steam off her skin as it drifted past Onur. Simultaneous chills and small electric shocks seemed to reach toward him from her, but he remained quiet and soon it passed and Ann calmed down.

I hope I know what the fuck I'm doing and she doesn't rip me apart on accident.

"What do you think about tomorrow?"

CHAPTER 16

Nius watched as the sun began its slow morning climb towards the sky. Fingers of light caressed his face as he leaned against the brick behind him. His breathing came heavy and his eyes threatened to close against his will as exhaustion from sleepless nights accumulated.

No matter how hard he tried or how much he did, it felt like he was pushing a boulder up a mountain of sand. The majority of his time was now spent stopping small robberies. Almost all of the robberies were desperate men and women looking for something to feed their families as the city collapsed.

"What do you do when the bread and butter of thieves is actual bread and butter to survive?" He made a mental note to ask Terry the next time he saw the priest.

At least no more kidnappings. He tried to remain

optimistic and see the silver lining. He had very little idea as to why the late-night abductions had stopped. Though it would have been nice to feel like he had made a change, he seriously doubted it had stopped because of him.

The strangest desire to keep moving returned. It was an anxiousness that made his legs bounce restlessly. Over the last few days, Nius had been left with an uneasy feeling of being watched. He had taken to looking over his shoulder often.

Though exhausted, these open rooftops were no place to rest. Nius shouldered his backpack and tightened the straps to ensure it stayed on. He made his way to the edge and peered down at the ridiculous drop that stretched below him. Tiny dots meandered on streets that looked like thin gray ribbons from this height. He stepped lightly off the skyscraper, tumbling over and over as the air whipped past. He enjoyed the rise in his stomach as he flipped through the air. As the ground rushed up to embrace him, Nius shifted his body until he fell feet first.

His plummet slowed a few feet off the ground and he touched down in the dark space between buildings. He spun on the spot as the overwhelming sensation of being watched shook him again. The alley remained empty, though, and Nius felt silly at his reaction.

You're just tired and paranoid and jumping at shadows. He wished he believed that.

Making his way out of the alley and onto a main street, Nius melted into the crowd and disappeared into the mass of happy shoppers.

Any relief he gained by blending in was shattered almost immediately by a scream of fear.

A roaring engine and squealing tires rose above the noise as a car careened erratically down the main street. The car's wheels bounced up onto the sidewalk nearly killing a dozen pedestrians as they fled in all directions.

"How in the hell do I stop that?"

Knowing full well he had no hope of stopping the car, he noticed a man frozen in the car's path.

Move. He hoped they would get out of the way.

"Move!" But still the person did not budge.

Nius shot off towards him, desperation feeding his will as his muscles and body gave everything he asked. He fired across the sidewalk, navigating around people with such grace and fluidity they felt only his breeze. Nius scooped him up over a shoulder and continued until he reached the sidewalk. Setting him down again, Nius looked him over to make sure he was all right. The man's gaze unsettled him.

He had expected terror or relief. Maybe even gratitude, but the man watched him with hawk-like focus. It was a gaze that penetrated and calculated and it felt intrusive for someone like Nius, who'd been raised to hide himself. Nius focused back on the car.

Without a trace of erratic swerving, the large black vehicle sped off before taking the corner like a racer and roaring off into the distance.

Nius focused energy again as he bent his knees to sprint after the car.

"Wait!" the rescued man shouted. "I need to talk to you."

Nius paused. "And I need to stop that car."

"But it was after me. It's me they are trying to kill!"

Nius stood back up. The stranger had his attention.

"I need your help, young man. Please, take my card."

Nius took the small paper rectangle and began to reply when the ground was shaken by an explosion further up the street.

"What is it with this city?" Nius cried out in exasperation. He turned back to the stranger but the man was gone.

*

Herod could scarcely believe the difference between his expectations and the reality he had seen. The teenager had appeared exhausted and with dark bags forming under his eyes, dressed in torn clothing.

How does a bastion of power I can scarcely understand look like a teenage heroin addict? Regardless of the kid's condition, Herod had seen what he could do.

Dozens of squad cars blew past the nearby parked vehicle he had entered. Their sirens blared as they rushed in the same direction the boy had headed. Eruptions of distant gunfire reached him as people deserted the streets with screams.

"What in the hell is happening near Chocolat Couvert?" he demanded into his line.

"We got them sir, we have the hacker and girl trapped under suppressive fire."

"Listen to me. Capture her now but do not under any circumstances let her die. The other kid is headed in your direction and this is your top priority. Do *not* let him make contact with them."

"What?"

"Scare off the kid. Capture the girl. But do not let them make contact. That is your utmost goal."

"What do we do about the hacker?"

"Kill him. With him gone, this all becomes a lot easier."

CHAPTER 17

"So sorry! It's packed today!" The waitress shouted her apology over the din as she jostled past Onur. She had bumped his arm hard enough for coffee to dribble down and stain his shirt.

He gave her a noncommittal grunt and continued staring into the mug. He had yet to take a sip.

"Ordering coffee to blend in doesn't work if it looks like you're thinking about drowning yourself in it," Ann muttered from across the table.

He made a face at her and grabbed a napkin, wiping at his shirt front.

They sat in a booth by the window of the coffee shop, just across the street from the brothel Onur had decided to try to use to look for Jim's family. Onur's nerves were a wreck as he studied the brothel through the glass. He tried to work out a layout or plan but had no idea what was in there except a big trap.

Ann sat quietly enjoying her caramel and caffeine concoction. She seemed to be enjoying the atmosphere in the coffee shop.

I suppose if I could toss cars like toys, I wouldn't be so nervous. But the excuse didn't ring true. He hadn't been nearly this nervous when breaking into the warehouse.

Ann smirked at the look he gave her, and despite himself, he grinned. She smiled back. He felt an affectionate tug on his heart and the rush of worry returned with force.

"I'm not worried about me. I'm worried about her," he whispered.

"What are you worried about?" she leaned in to ask. Onur was shocked she had heard but redirected the conversation.

"The plan. Want to hear it?"

"Tell me."

Onur leaned toward her conspiratorially. "Stage one is super simple. That place is airtight all over, which means I have to get them to open the door. I walk up, I knock like I'm looking for some pay-to-play and Alton sneaks in. Once in, he can pinpoint where we need to hit so we aren't wasting time running around that place. And you can stay here. As backup."

Ann looked unhappy.

"There is nothing to it and we don't need to put anyone in danger or anything."

She still seemed upset and Onur could guess why.

"At least until stage two. That shit's dangerous and all you, girl." Ann looked happier at the mention of stage two.

Onur took a deep breath, rose from the booth and slipped his backpack on. He gave Ann a nervous wink as he attempted confidence.

"Hm. It's kind of hard to look alpha and self-assured with a coffee stain, huh?" she asked.

"Yeah. It's the stain. *That's* the problem. Not the trembling wreck behind it," he joked as he took one last glance at her before leaving. Her mirth and smile were gone and replaced with genuine worry as she watched him go.

Onur's hands trembled as he made his way out the door with a churning stomach. He watched as a middle-aged man approached the large metal door of the brothel. The man gave a few knocks and moments later it opened and he entered.

Just like everyone else has.

Waiting for the crosswalk light to change felt like an eternity and his fingers twitched with nervous energy. His watch gave an annoyed buzz to discourage the behavior.

"Sorry, Alton. It's nerves." The light changed and Onur started the march across the street with heart beating so hard he thought he might choke.

This isn't even the hard part. I'm just getting Alton in, he reminded himself.

As he approached the large and uninviting steel door, he felt Alton unclasp from his wrist as the small robot readied itself. Onur knocked once and waited until the door cracked open. Slightly suspicious eyes questioned him.

"I was hoping to get laid?"

A muscular arm shot through the door grabbing the front of his shirt and jerking him inside before slamming the exit shut.

"That isn't the right knock."

"There's a secret knock? What is this, a fucking kids' clubhouse?" he asked frantically as his plan was thrown into chaos.

In response, the man pulled back a fist and bashed Onur in the face.

Onur saw stars and a burst of pain from a now-split lip. He held his face and tried to stop the bleeding.

"Who do you work for?" the security demanded and cocked a fist back for another punch.

"You shouldn't have done that," Onur warned through gritted teeth.

"Why? You going to do something about it?" The large man sneered but Onur just shook his head no.

"She has abandonment issues, you asshole."

The burly security furrowed his brow in confusion. "What?"

A tremendous blow shook the building, causing concrete dust to spill down from the ceiling. The guard's surprise was complete when he saw the sturdy steel door warped badly and bubbling inward. Another tremor shook the building and the warped steel slab jerked from its hinges and toppled into the room. Behind it stood Ann.

The guard just stuttered, unable to process what was happening. Ann lifted the twisted metal door and whipped it towards the man, allowing him a much closer look at it before it crushed him into the wall.

"Are you ok?" Her question was drowned out as the building erupted into ear-splitting alarms.

"I'm fine," Onur yelled over the alarms. "But the plan went to shit and now we improvise."

At least a dozen security members had rushed the lobby. Some carried assault rifles and all carried batons. Ann ripped the metal door free of the wall and slung it towards the group. A few lucky ones managed to duck and avoid the spinning metal, but most were cut down like wheat.

Onur noticed one of the men on the ground readying his rifle with sights on Ann. He dug through his hip pack and struck the man squarely in the face with a small metal sphere. Jerking uncontrollably, the man slumped, blood leaking from his mouth where he had likely bitten through his tongue. One of the others charged wildly, swinging the dense baton at Ann's head. Her hand snatched the weapon, and her grip bent the polycarbonate material, squeezing through her fingers like modeling clay. Ann ripped it from his grasp before slapping him across the head with it.

With the lobby security dealt with, Onur rushed deeper into the brothel.

"Time, girl! We don't have any!"

With Ann following and Alton flying ahead somewhere, Onur wondered where they kept the access console. The brothel was a dizzying building with dozens of private rooms along a corridor. With a sudden thought Onur stopped. The tripped alarm seemed to have initiated a lockdown on some of the doors here. They were clearly designed to protect something.

Something possibly important.

"Can you get into some of these? As many as you can? They might even be in here right now." Without a word, Ann turned towards the nearest bedroom and punched through the panic door as screams erupted from inside. Ann tossed the door to the side.

A young woman huddled in the corner of the room naked and terrified as Ann stepped in. On the bed sat a trembling older man digging through his wallet and offering wads of cash.

"Here! Take it! Take it all. Just don't hurt me. I have a wife and kids!"

Ann stared him down. "Then why are you here?"

The man had no answer so Ann turned to the frightened young girl. "Were you kidnapped?" The girl nodded, her eyes streaming tears.

"Go. Get dressed and get out of here." Ann turned back to Onur. "You realize I have to open them all now."

"Alton's got the terminal. Second floor. But for all I know, they could be locked in one of these rooms. You keep checking and I'll go find the access point."

"I'll be there soon."

Onur took off towards the stairwell as he listened to the twisting of metal behind him.

Taking the steps three at a time, he rushed up the dark stairwell. Emergency lights filled the concrete stairs with red light. He reached the top and moved for the door, hoping it remained open. Onur peered through, checking the empty top floor.

"Ann must have taken care of them all in the lobby."

The dimly lit corridor was lined with doors that had not shut with the security alarm. Wandering past the open doorways, Onur peered into the empty rooms wondering why these had no customers or clients.

A door at the end of the long corridor held a large sign: **Employees only. All others will be killed on sight.**

"Subtle." The door was slightly ajar and Onur gave it a small push. He nearly choked. Surrounded by video monitors and server banks, a table at the center of the room served as a cash counting area. Mountains of green bills had been in the process of being organized and banded into stacks before Onur and Ann's entrance must have interrupted. Onur stared agape at the fortune in front of him. He was completely oblivious even to Alton's chirps and tones as the small AI begged for help in breaking into the secure network.

"Ow, what the hell?" he demanded in pain as Alton slammed into the side of his head.

The small flying robot chittered angrily in response until Onur checked the message on his phone.

<Unable to access main console. Physical security is preventing my connection>

"Yeah, yeah. I'll break us in but you search and upload what we need. And no more Steel Jitsu on me. You are hard." Rubbing the welt on his head, he set to work. Pulling a small pry bar from his pack, he inserted the edge into a crack and pried open the panel, giving Alton access to its inner circuitry and boards. Checking his phone again, he noticed the AI had linked him a status gauge. The slowly filling bar indicated how much data Alton still needed to download.

The building shook again accompanied by an angry scream.

"You assholes!" He heard Ann yell from outside in the hall.

Another loud bang sounded from the stairwell. Onur peeked his head out and saw Ann in front of the stairwell door holding the steel door shut against the banging of many men.

"Oh, did you bring us some company?" Onur grinned but stopped when he saw the look of terror Ann wore.

"They have bombs. It's not going to be long before they use them on this door."

"Shit, almost done!" He ducked back into the room where Alton was waiting. Checking his phone, he saw status was complete.

He looked again at the money, his hand already unzipping his backpack.

"You better hurry because they stopped banging!" Ann warned from the corridor.

Onur ignored the guilt and shoved stacks of hundreds into every available pocket and pouch of his backpack.

He heard another explosion and Ann staggered into the room.

“You ok?”

“They missed me,” she said with a grin of blood-stained teeth and trickle of blood running down her face into her eye. She wiped it away.

“Well, mostly. But the stairwell is full and elevators aren’t working.”

“I’m not dying stuck in a brothel.”

Grabbing her hand, Onur tugged Ann into the nearest bedroom. He nodded towards the window, which looked down into the alley. Typing into his cellphone, Onur held up a small shocking sphere and Alton zipped past, grabbing it on his way.

Ann looked around, grabbed the heavy steel bed frame, and heaved it through the glass.

Alton zipped out the broken window ahead of them.

Onur poked his head out the window and was pleased when he saw the squad car below. The bed frame had crushed one of the men and Alton shocked the other officer unconscious. Wasting little time, he pulled a thin climbing rope with a hook from his fanny pack. Onur secured the hook against the window frame and tossed the rope slack out.

"After you." He hurried her and started down right after. Onur dropped down next to her before scooping up one of the officer's hats and placing it on his head.

"And now we escape." He signaled for her to get in the car and duck as he slid into the driver's seat.

"I didn't expect it to be this easy to get away."

"Well, I don't have a driver's license and I've never driven so . . ."

"What?"

"You never need to in the city!"

The engine roared alive and Onur struggled with shifting into drive before performing an extremely jerky pull out onto the main street congested by police officers.

"Now we sneak away and the idiots aren't the wiser . . ." He chuckled before being interrupted by the car radio crackling to life.

"Car 300, report your position and destination. All cars called for an APB. Do not leave your current location and please report."

Shit . . . Onur's hopes dwindled.

"Captain. Car 300 leaving premises and not responding. We are awaiting orders."

A small pause was shattered by an order.

"Per the chief, fire on car 300 at will. Take out tires."

Onur hit the gas, revving the engine as the car

tires screeched and took off. The sounds of gunfire directed at their vehicle terrified him. He ducked down while trying to keep the speeding vehicle straight. As the burst of bullets shredded their tires, he lost control and the squad car veered wildly before slamming into a light pole.

CHAPTER 18

Onur woke to being shaken, his mouth filled with blood and the taste of pennies. They shook him again with more urgency as his brain tried to orient itself. His current predicament came back to him like an explosion in his mind. Sprawled across the front seats of the police car, Onur lay still. He could hear the engine hissing from under the hood of the dying vehicle.

We hit the post and . . . here we are. Ann shook again and Onur responded if just to stop her.

"Yes, Ann, shake the accident victim." He groaned sarcastically. A small relieved laugh escaped her.

"How long was I out?"

"What?" she asked, "It just happened, I didn't even know you were knocked out."

"We aren't all made of what you are," he remarked, sitting up to look at her before wishing he had not said it. Her light blond hair was streaked with her own blood, cuts and scratches peppering her face and oozing.

"Never mind, sorry."

"If it makes you feel any better, you look much worse than I do."

"No. I feel no better at all, thanks." He checked himself over, moving extremities and feeling for anything broken or no longer functional.

"That doesn't look good," he muttered, eyeing a blood-soaked spot on his shirt just above his right hip. He reached down, prodding as gently as he could.

"Oohhh fuck. Doesn't look good and feels so much worse." He hissed his breath through his teeth. With the thought of impending death came sudden clarity. The reason the police weren't firing at them was because they wanted Ann alive.

The things Herod would achieve, the awful things he would force her to do if that happened, proved too much.

"So . . . I got shot," he mentioned casually.

"What?" she demanded in disbelief. "Oh my god!"

"This is it, Ann. You have to run, okay? Herod wants you alive and I am assuming they aren't in a hurry to approach the car because they are chickenshit of you."

"I'm not going anywhere, are you kidding me?"

"I'm done, don't you get it? Herod can't get his hands on you. That's number one. You matter so much more than me. You've got to stay far away from him. So here's what I want you to do. Count to five, then kick the other door out and run like hell," Onur demanded forcefully.

Gritting his teeth, he reached for the handle near his feet while biting back a yell. Pushing with his legs, he opened the door, slowly and ungracefully scooching out of the car while trying not to pass out. With feet on the concrete and facing the horde of hundreds, he found he could not bear to look at Ann.

"Run faster than you ever have, Ann, or you're going to wish for death every day of your life." He gave her a sideways smile and tossed his phone towards her. "Take care of Alton, he likes you."

Grabbing the money-filled bag, he strapped it on and charged towards the officers, each step spearing him with agony. "Congratulations, Herod, you asshole," he muttered.

Gunfire rang out as hundreds of weapons unleashed what one could have accomplished.

He felt only the same pain from before.

Why does death feel exactly the same . . . ? Must be hell. Onur winched his eyelids open. He was grasping at anything to try to understand what had happened.

Standing between him and hundreds of officers with weapons drawn was a young man Onur had never seen before.

The cops shuffled uneasily as they moved back behind cover and cars. Their fear and nerves regarding this kid was open and obvious to Onur. It dawned on him. *You must be the other one I've been hearing about . . .*

"You want to do this again?" the teen shouted fiercely at the gathered force. Onur was stunned by his calm at hundreds of powerful rifles being aimed at him.

"Thank you . . ." Onur murmured.

"Don't thank me yet." The kid stopped him. "I don't know your place in all this, but judging by the state of that building and your bag stuffed with money, I'm not optimistic."

Onur shut his mouth.

"But I know for a fact these guys are the worst." The teenager jerked his head toward the cops and then reached back and offered Onur a hand up.

Onur gladly grabbed it and then instantly regretted the move as pain from his gut blasted through him and grew more intense as strange, hot, tingling energy flooded Onur. The bullet wound momentarily gushed more blood. Healthy tissue spread in place impossibly fast, filling the hole as it pushed the bullet out.

Onur stared wide-eyed and for once had no words.

"Go."

With his strength somewhat returned, Onur wasted

no time, snatching the money bag and turning for the ruined vehicle. Ann stood on the other side of the crashed squad car, her face unreadable and focused on the kid.

"What are you waiting for?" he shouted. "Run!"

There was no sign from Ann that she even saw or heard him.

Darkness seeped from her now black eyes.

*

Nius watched the girl with black eyes cross the distance between them in a heartbeat. Her hand thrust out for his throat, making apparent contact an inch away from his skin. She squeezed with enough force to crush steel and slammed him into the blacktop. Pinning him down by the neck with one arm, she punched viciously with her other. Nius felt his head sink into the shattering pavement beneath as his protection held against the onslaught.

The girl grunted in obvious frustration.

Nius punched her throat, loosening her grip. As she choked for breath, Nius used the opportunity to roll back and launch himself away from her.

She leaped at him again, but he was not so unprepared. She smashed her fist toward his head, but Nius ducked backwards under the blow and kicked into her stomach. She grabbed for his hair, but her hand was deflected. She had a handful of nothing and was launched backward through the brothel's thick brick walls.

Though every fiber of Nius's being screamed at him to run, he leapt through the hole, following her into the darkness.

CHAPTER 19

Onur jumped and slid across the trunk of the crashed squad car, rolling off the other side to safety.

A thunderous boom rang out from inside the brothel and a section of outside wall collapsed, sending dust rushing out of windows and doors.

"This is insane!" he screamed in the din. He poked at the odd scar in his side that had been a bleeding bullet wound only moments ago. Onur could scarcely believe what he had seen in just the last few minutes, including Ann's unexplainable meltdown. Why had she attacked the kid like that after he'd helped them?

Without warning, Ann burst through a window in the brothel and shattered glass blew everywhere. Onur watched in shock as she spun quickly in midair, landing on all fours and clawing deep gouges in the concrete with her fingers. With onyx black eyes she was unrecognizable as the girl Onur had been laughing at TV shows with the past few nights. He tried to get her attention, but no luck.

The kid who'd stopped the bullets hopped out the window after Ann, but was knocked off balance when she launched herself back at him, tackling him in the stomach and into the building once again.

"She moves like a wild animal." Onur was baffled at what he was seeing in Ann.

Renewed gunfire behind him forced him to duck.

"I guess with her not around, I'm priority." The hopeless feeling from moments ago returned. With the kid and Ann fighting, he was alone out here, surrounded by Herod's bought-and-paid-for officers who would kill first and ask questions never. The rounds came quicker as the cops moved closer.

Onur frantically tried to think of an escape, panic making him hyperventilate. A bullet nearly missed taking his shoulder off. The loud chaos slipped away as Onur sank into his mind, his fingers working his cellphone in a blur.

*

Reclining in one of Fenicia's pump stations, the city worker cracked another beer, caring little for the responsibilities of watching over the water system for the huge city. Mostly automated and connected to similar water stations all over Fenny, the huge pumps that kept the city watered generally ran themselves. He noticed his shift partner passed out midway through his dirty magazine.

"Learn to hold your beer, man. Jeez," he chided.

Draining his own bottle and leaning back for the last drops, his chair shifted hard and he fell backward.

"What the—" he gasped.

With no prompting, the three tremendous water pumps had roared to life. Automated valves and shut-offs throughout the facility either screeched open or ground shut, redirecting water.

"Kurt! KURT!" he yelled, jumping to his feet and running towards the controls. The pumps roared louder and louder as their power was increased.

"What the hell did you do? The pumps were never meant to run this hard! You're going to break them!" he hollered over the furious noise of millions of gallons of seawater being forced into the city's water system.

"I didn't do anything, come over here and fix it!"

Sitting down at the controls, the man felt like he was going to vomit. He turned back to his partner. "All three stations are doing this. Automated shut-offs were killed, and the pumps are running full power. All this water is being directed to one spot." He tapped at the keys but nothing happened. "I'm locked out. I can't shut anything off or open anything up! HO-LEE SHIT! This city was built to need way more water than it does now. I wish Noah and his ark were here because these water mains are going to build in pressure until something blows, and when it does, it's going to be a flood!"

*

A deafening siren rang out through the city, familiar to all the citizens. The warning system had been installed for potential tsunamis or earthquakes. The shrieking alarm was followed by a voice blaring across the city urging citizens to reach higher ground and safety.

The cops stopped firing and looked around uneasily as the warning rang through the streets. Watching the scene from his large black sedan, behind the sea of police cars, Herod grew angry.

"They are to stay put," he demanded of the police chief in the front passenger seat next to Norm. "Idiots . . . It's that goddamn hacker."

The alarm continued but the command to stay put had been issued. Heeding the order and not knowing what else to do they aimed their weapons at the crash.

In a moment, small vibrations could be felt through the ground. They were almost imperceptible until police cars began shaking and rocking. Without a word, Herod and his company jumped out of their vehicle and ran into the nearest building. They vaulted up the stairs, followed by some officers who thought better of staying put.

Suddenly, manholes exploded like bottle caps atop intense plumes of pressurized water. With a deafening roar, the wall of seawater crashed through, carrying cars and officers with it, before hitting Onur like an unyielding bulwark of a ship and dragging him away under the waves. Onur reached up through the dark dirty water towards the fading sunlight, but the current overtook him, leaving him spinning like a toy in a river.

CHAPTER 20

Nius stared through the wreckage of the floor to the lower level and the fear inside him grew like a shrill scream in the back of his mind. Dark and lightless, the basement he had kicked the girl into revealed nothing. Her strength was immense, each of her blows sending shocks through his spine and skin, testing his protection to its limits.

Is this who Terry was talking about? "Not bad?" he muttered, questioning the priest's description of the girl.

The words had barely left his mouth before the wall behind him exploded. The girl tore through the brick, her momentum carrying them both to the opposite wall and embedding Nius into the drywall. The girl's hand shot towards Nius's face but again his protections prevented her fist from reaching its destination. Any relief Nius felt about this vanished as black mist erupted from her fingertips, the mist shot through with crackles of energy. Nius watched in horror as fissures appeared in the air where her power began to pierce his barrier. He grabbed her wrist but could not hope to break the strength of her grip. Without warning, familiar blue light limned his hand, spreading from his fingers to her skin. Her black eyes widened in surprise as her grip loosened and he took advantage of the moment. Able to lift both legs while she held him up, Nius kicked her in the stomach and against the opposite wall.

It was her manner that bothered him. She acted like a feral animal, her attacks single-minded hate focused on his destruction.

Run . . . The warning came with flashes of churning white rapids, cars and people caught in vicious currents, but the images made little sense to him.

The building shook with a deafening roar of rushing water and screams, and what appeared to be the ocean began flowing past the upper floor windows and soaked them to their ankles.

What the heck?

Nius sprinted towards the window but stopped when he noticed her matching his movement—but towards him rather than any attempt to escape. The screams went on, and Nius's heart ached for the people in the flood he could not help, the ache becoming frustration.

“Your friend is out there,” Nius said, hoping to penetrate her single-minded fixation on him. “I fixed his gunshot but unless he can swim like hell, he will die.”

The words seemed to make no difference at first, and Nius was prepared for another attempt at fending off strangulation, but then her body finally relaxed. She looked at him, confused, eyes filled with regret and fear of loss.

Such beautiful brown eyes.

In a second, she was gone, leaping out the window and into the furious water.

*

Onur’s lungs were on fire. He tried to hold onto his last breath but was slammed into a light post, and the air was knocked out of him with the pain forces of the impact. Dizzy and not knowing which way was up, he thrashed about in vain, until a hand grabbed the back of his shirt and dragged him through the rushing water.

Ann held him while kicking through the floodwaters and holding his face up above the waves.

Ha, she’s a mermaid! thought Onur, and then all went black.

If you enjoyed this book, please consider leaving a review at your favorite book retailer. Enthusiastic reviews from readers are vital to authors everywhere. Your support is greatly appreciated!

Made in the USA
Monee, IL
02 September 2021

77142817R10167